"Open Your Eyes, Dianna."

She shook her head.

"Open them, I want to see you," he ordered softly, and she obeyed.

"Do you love me? Is that why you agreed to marry me?"

Her eyes were blank; the question had not registered.

"Answer me, Dianna. Do you love me?"

"Yes." She closed her eyes and pulled his lips toward hers, catching only a glimpse of his victorious smile.

"Then let me love you." He picked her up and carried her to the bed. . . .

RITA CLAY

has tried almost every job once. This former book-store manager also sold cosmetics, worked in a bank and ran her own modeling school before turning to writing. Now a successful romance author, she looks forward to describing the diversity and joys of love in many books to come.

Dear Reader:

SILHOUETTE DESIRE is an exciting new line of contemporary romances from Silhouette Books. During the past year, many Silhouette readers have written in telling us what other types of stories they'd like to read from Silhouette, and we've kept these comments and suggestions in mind in developing SILHOUETTE DESIRE.

DESIREs feature all of the elements you like to see in a romance, plus a more sensual, provocative story. So if you want to experience all the excitement, passion and joy of falling in love, then SILHOUETTE DESIRE is for you.

I hope you enjoy this book and all the wonderful stories to come from SILHOUETTE DESIRE. I'd appreciate any thoughts you'd like to share with us on new SILHOUETTE DESIRE, and I invite you to write to us at the address below:

Karen Solem
Editor-in-Chief
Silhouette Books
P.O. Box 769
New York, N.Y. 10019

RITA CLAY
Wise Folly

Silhouette Desire
Published by Silhouette Books New York
America's Publisher of Contemporary Romance

Other Silhouette Books by Rita Clay

Wanderer's Dream

SILHOUETTE BOOKS, a Simon & Schuster Division of
GULF & WESTERN CORPORATION
1230 Avenue of the Americas, New York, N.Y. 10020

Copyright © 1982 by Rita Clay

Distributed by Pocket Books

ISBN: 0-671-44372-0

First Silhouette Books printing June, 1982

10 9 8 7 6 5 4 3 2 1

America's Publisher of Contemporary Romance

Printed in the U.S.A.

To My Cousin, Ruthann,
For Reading, Reading, and Reading

1

Dianna's eyes widened appreciatively as she glanced around the executive reception area of Wescomp, Inc. The changes since she had been here last were dramatic. The interior was now decorated in a contemporary style featuring soft colors, fluorescent lighting, and an abundance of live plants. The carpeting was a deep forest green, the walls a paler shade of the same color. Bright modern paintings reflected off the glass partitions and brought all the tones together in harmony. The total look was relaxed but efficient.

A young girl sat at the receptionist's desk filing her nails with wholehearted dedication. Preoccupied with her task, she hadn't noticed Dianna's entrance. The telephone intercom buzzed loudly and the girl jumped, then jumped again when she noticed the tall, well-dressed woman standing in front of her. Dianna's lips twitched in a smile, the girl's almost comical nervousness helping dispel some of her own.

"Oh, I'm sorry! Hold on a minute, won't you?" she asked, all composure gone as she fidgeted with the buttons of the intercom. Dianna watched the girl's confusion for a moment before she calmly reached over and flipped one of the switches to the "on" position, earning a grateful smile.

"I guess you can tell this isn't my regular job. I'm usually in the typing pool, but Mr. Bradshaw's secretary was sick today and they pulled me in to help." She picked up the receiver. "Yes, Mr. Bradshaw?" she asked sweetly in a sing-song voice while making a face into the phone. "Mrs. Hammond?" Dianna nodded in confirmation. "Yes, sir, she's here. I was just about to ring you, sir." Then there was a moment's hesitation. "Yes, sir."

She cradled the receiver gently. "Boy, is he in a foul mood! Watch out, Mrs. Hammond—even on his nice days he's nothing to brag about." The young girl swished her long hair over her shoulders and glanced appraisingly at the other woman's cream-colored suit and silk black-bowed blouse. Her dark hair was in a soft but business-like French pleat. She looked stunning, the young girl decided—more than a match for the formidable Mr. Bradshaw.

Dianna smiled her thanks and walked into the office, a much larger room than the reception area. Mr. Bradshaw sat behind a rather well worn desk, bifocals perched on a hawklike nose, his eyes peering over both. "Mrs. Hammond? Have a seat, please." He indicated a chair, his voice high but raspy. His hand patted the few remaining hairs on his balding head as he gave her a puzzled smile. Obviously he had expected someone older than she appeared. She took a seat, gracefully sitting back in the dark leather chair.

"Please excuse me for being surprised, Mrs. Hammond. The people down in Personnel recommended you highly, but I had the impression you would be older. I didn't realize you would be such an assured and beautiful young woman," he said, aware of being caught staring and faintly embarrassed. Her appearance explained many of his unanswered questions.

"Surely looks don't have much to do with qualifications, Mr. Bradshaw?" she murmured.

"Of course not! It's just that we seldom have applicants who are both experienced *and* easy on the eyes."

Dianna gave a small laugh as she opened her briefcase and pulled out her resume, handing it to him. "Thank you, but as you can see, I'm twenty-eight years old and have seven years' experience in the computer field."

He quickly scanned her credentials, placing one neatly typed page behind the other until he finished all four pages. The dull sounds of traffic far below mingled with the soft ticking of the wall clock behind his desk as she apprehensively watched the expression flitting across his face. Apparently he was impressed with what he read, for a small satisfied smile tugged at his craggy features.

"Excellent!" he said as he set the resume down on his desk and sat back in his leather chair. "Congratulations, Mrs. Hammond. I want to welcome you to Wescomp as our new head of Programming."

The job was hers, and the salary Mr. Bradshaw

mentioned was better than she had anticipated! In two weeks time she would officially start working at Wescomp, Inc. The choice had been made and now the matter was out of her hands. She was no longer tense or upset. She only hoped it would all turn out for the best.

As the interview closed Dianna gave a small resigned sigh, leaning forward in her chair to reach for the necessary forms that she would have to fill out and return.

Mr. Bradshaw glanced down at the resume, a surprised look flitting across his face. "I must have missed this the first time, Mrs. Hammond. You're a widow and you have a child of six?"

"Yes. My husband died several years ago—just before Tabby was born," she lied calmly. It was a story she had repeated so often she almost felt it was the truth.

"I see. And you married a cousin?" he asked, looking at her with hard piercing eyes magnified by his bifocals.

"Why do you say that?"

"Because our records show your maiden name to be Hammond also."

For just a fleeting second Dianna sat immobilized, her head spinning for an answer. Her few friends hadn't known her before Tabby, so she had never run into the problem before. Grasping at the straw he had thrown, she smiled. "Oh . . . yes. Although he was a very distant cousin."

He seemed to ponder this awhile before accepting it with a nod. Then he reached back into the bottom drawer and pulled out more carboned forms. "You'll want your daughter on the medical insurance also—am I correct?"

"Yes. That was one of my main reasons for reapplying to Wescomp. I want Tabby to have the best, should she ever need it." Dianna stood and accepted the added forms with a feeling of relief before holding out her hand.

"Thank you for your time."

He shook hands, and then, just as she reached the door, he called, "By the way, Mrs. Hammond. A week from tomorrow there will be a cocktail party in honor of the installation of our new computer. All our major stockholders and the department heads are to attend. Though you won't start work until a week after the party, I'd like you to come. It will give you a chance to meet some of the people you'll be working with." He gave a strained smile as if anticipating her reluctance even before she had a chance to react. "All part of the job, you know."

She hesitated. "May I pass on it?"

"I'm sorry, but it's imperative you attend. After all, these are the people who keep our corporation growing."

"Very well, and thank you again," Dianna said, acquiescing.

She closed the door quietly and leaned against its frame for just a moment. Funny how composed she had been, when she'd thought she would be nervous. Just seven years ago her feelings had been very different when a position at Wescomp was offered her. Then she had been excited and hopeful. Just out of college and eager to embark on a business career, she had thought the job at Wescomp a dream come true. She had never guessed how quickly that dream would become a nightmare.

Her high heels echoed with a businesslike click as she made her way down the corridor toward the elevator. She'd been in Mr. Bradshaw's office for almost an hour and had never noticed that the light on his intercom panel had been lit all that time. . . .

There was a feeling of relief in having the position with Wescomp. Leaving the job she had held for the past seven years with a smaller computer company had been a major step, but now it was done. And because of Wescomp, Tabby would have the advantages she deserved: clothing, medical care, and a few more hours a week to spend with her mother.

Tabby. She was the one source of pleasure in her mother's life, and whenever Dianna thought of her she felt a sense of accomplishment. She was all a six-year-old girl should be. Small for her age, she was a beautiful miniature of her mother, with the exception of her warm gray eyes and caramel-colored hair. Tabby was impish and loving, an indefinable blend of sober adult and mischievous child. And now, both she and Tabby had two wonderful weeks in which to relax before getting into the routine of work once more.

The late June days in Dallas were warm and balmy, and Dianna and Tabby made the most of them by taking small side trips through the countryside. They went to Livingston and visited the Alabama–Coushatta Indian Reservation deep in the heart of the tall pine country. Another time they drove down to the Galveston coast, renting a small gaily striped pink-and-white tent. They spent the day in its shade as they listened to the waves rush back and forth against the sandy shore. It served as a lullaby for Tabby, who slept better than she had in weeks, waking with rested eyes, flushed cheeks, and more energy than she'd displayed in a long time.

They enjoyed it, but all the time there was a niggling worry in the back of Dianna's mind. The cocktail party for Wescomp was closer with every passing day, and she was dreading it all out of proportion. It wasn't necessary for a computer programmer to have the expertise of a socialite, she told herself in calmer moments. Just because she had not dated since Tabby was born she certainly wasn't such a country bumpkin that she couldn't converse intelligently with other people! After all, what was she expecting to happen? No one knew of her past, and she shouldn't let it hinder her future. If she was tense, it was her own fault. She was making something out of nothing, she told herself. Then she would halt in midthought. Coming face to face with Noah Weston was *not* nothing!

The Friday of the cocktail party was also the appointed day for Tabby's visit to the specialist. They walked into his office and began the necessary but familiar examination. Dianna smiled brightly, telling herself it was all right, nothing had changed. But it had, a small voice taunted, and the knowledge caused a tight ball of frustration in the pit of her stomach. She kept looking at the specialist, a tall spare man with eyes that seemed to see through the body without the help of X rays, hoping for a clue. He gave none. Tabby was given a complete checkup, then handed a teen magazine to read in the lobby while her mother talked to Dr. Storn. Tabby had misgivings about missing the best part of the conversation and left reluctantly, taking one of the uncomfortable straight-backed chairs in the reception room.

Dianna's eyes rested on the doctor's downbent head,

wondering why he wasn't smiling as much as he had after the last visit. A small thread of fear wound its way around her heart as the minutes ticked by. She knew what he was going to say. She knew. . . .

"Is it so much worse, Doctor?" she asked, her remark more a statement than a question. He glanced up, his thoughts brought back to the worried woman in front of him and out of the pages of a young child's heart history.

"Yes, Mrs. Hammond. We can't delay much longer. She needs surgery as soon as possible," he stated grimly. "You've seen the change in the past weeks?" She nodded her head, afraid her voice had failed, tears brimming in her eyes. Her mind had shut out the possibility of change, but she had known deep down that Tabby was weakening.

"Yes, I've noticed. I'm in the process of changing jobs and I've taken a small vacation, keeping a closer eye on her than usual. She's tired by midmorning and her color is so pale she almost looks blue. She's not sleeping well either."

"I'd say with luck we may have another month. After that . . ." He shrugged his shoulders. "This isn't a thing you can point to and say 'in two weeks,' or 'in three days' time.' Every day is a gift. I just hope that by the time we're ready for surgery she'll be strong enough to endure the operation."

He bent forward, his elbows on his knees as he took both her hands in his. She looked down at his massive hands, hands that could do such intricate surgery, and was surprised at their gentleness.

"I know," she choked. "I want this medical plan to go into effect. Then we can proceed as planned."

"And in case surgery is needed before then?" he asked softly but insistently, squeezing her hands lightly.

"Then we'll have it done before." She glanced up to gaze into his face, her eyes showing the strength of steel behind the shiny tears. "Nothing must happen to her. Nothing."

He smiled slightly, admiring her for her determination, then cleared his throat and stood. "Give me a call if there's the slightest change." He turned briskly as he walked her toward the door and opened it for her to pass, giving a wink to the small golden-haired girl waiting impatiently outside. Tabby winked in response as she left the seat and took her mother's hand in hers.

"Bye." Tabby waved as she led her mother to the outside door, smiling at the doctor with a sweetness that could melt the most cynical of hearts.

All the way to June's house Dianna was preoccupied, barely listening to her daughter's chatter as they drove through the downtown traffic toward the suburban area. The land turned flat, without trees to soften the landscape or the Texas sun's burning rays as Dianna neared her sister's home. June had offered them the extra bedroom for the night so that she could care for Tabby while Dianna made her appearance at the cocktail party.

Two days ago Mr. Bradshaw had called to remind her of the reception and had stated that a car would be picking her up around five thirty that evening. Despite her protests that she could get there herself, he had been adamant about sending the car. His insistence had given Dianna an uneasy feeling that had been with her ever since.

They pulled into the drive and Tabby jumped out, eager to greet her cousins. There were few playmates her age near home and Tabby had no one to keep her company except for Mrs. Gurnig, an elderly neighbor who had watched her since she was a baby. Coming to Aunt June's was always a treat.

"Don't run, Tabby." Dianna's voice was sharper than she meant it to be, and she softened it with a smile as her daughter turned, surprised at her tone. "The doctor said that you should be taking it easy for a while," she explained, and Tabby nodded, looking much like a miniature adult in her seriousness. Dianna wanted to hug her, hold her close, but all she could do was nod her head and follow her to the door.

An hour later Dianna and June sat quietly over a fresh cup of coffee, the children playing a game in the front room. A small radio sat on the ledge of the kitchen window and sent out low sweet music, emphasizing the peaceful atmosphere.

Dianna sighed. "You're so lucky, June."

"Don't I know it!" She rubbed at an imaginary spot on the table. "If nothing else goes right all day, at least I know David will be home in the evening and listen to my woes. Sometimes he even makes me laugh over them." She smiled sweetly. It was a smile that showed the only resemblance between Dianna and June. June was much smaller than her sister, with a crop of short, dark brown wavy hair that seemed to have a mind of its own more often than not. By contrast, Dianna's long blue-black tresses hung past her shoulders when they weren't neatly arranged in a pleat. June's skin tone was different too, a light olive, while Dianna's complexion was a pale peach. Dianna pulled her robe tighter around her slim middle as she stretched back in her chair, attempting to relax the knotted nerves in her shoulder muscles.

June frowned as she watched. "What you need is a husband and more kids, Dianna. You're not really as career minded as you pretend to be."

"What should I do, take an ad in the paper? I can see it now! 'Unmarried mother wants rich husband to act as father and provide stud service.' No thanks! As far as I'm concerned David and your son will have to be the only men in my life." Her voice was bitter, but underlying the bitterness was fear. Pure fear.

"How one man could do so much damage, I don't know," June murmured as she eyed her sister worriedly. "You can't let it warp your whole life, Dianna. It's not fair!"

"In the past seven years I've learned not to trust men's motives. All they know when they see my child is that I climbed into bed once, so why shouldn't I do it again?" Dianna stood and walked to the kitchen door, her shoulders drooping wearily. "Besides, since when did anyone say life was fair?" she asked. "Just count your blessings, June, and I'll count mine. At least I've got Tabby."

"That's the most important thing," her sister agreed. "And now that you're working for Wescomp you'll be able to afford Tabby's operation, too. Seeing her strong and healthy again will be the biggest fringe benefit of all."

"I know," Dianna mused. "But somehow I can't shake this feeling of doom whenever I think about starting work there. I just hope to heaven that applying at Wescomp was the right thing to do."

"Of course it was, honey," June was quick to reassure her. "It's Noah Weston that's got you so nervous. Isn't it?" At Dianna's confirming nod, her sister shook her head in perplexity. "I just don't understand why that man scares you so! You should have gone to him seven years ago when you first found out you were pregnant and asked for his help, instead of waiting until now and going to his company for a job.''

"No! I don't ever want him to know about Tabby! I'd rather die than take his charity.''

Taken aback by Dianna's vehemence, June looked down at her hands a moment with a worried expression, then met her sister's gaze as if about to make a confession. "Dianna, I . . . I hope you won't be angry, but . . .''

"But what?'' she questioned tersely.

"I . . . oh, never mind. It's nothing really. Let me see about getting the children's dinner.'' June's uncharacteristically evasive words puzzled Dianna a moment, but she had too many other worries to spend time figuring out this new riddle.

A sleek steel gray Lincoln Continental purred up the residential street and stopped in front of June's door at exactly five o'clock that evening. A tall slim young man dressed in a black tuxedo walked up the pavement and knocked.

"Mrs. Hammond, please,'' he said, a smile lighting up his pleasant face as he looked after the fair-haired little girl who went off to get her mother.

"I hope I haven't kept you waiting,'' Dianna greeted him when she appeared a moment later, picking up the black lace shawl she had placed on the hall chair earlier. She bent and gave Tabby a kiss, not seeing the admiring glance of the young man waiting. Her simple black sheath was perfect for the occasion. It was a sleeveless vee-neck with an A-line skirt that swished when she moved and hugged her slim curves when she stood still, tastefully outlining the stunning figure she seemed so unaware of.

They didn't speak again until after he'd seated her in the luxurious car and slipped into the driver's seat. As he placed the car in gear and began to slowly drive away from the suburban community, he turned to her with a smile.

"By the way, my name is Jason Manners. I work at Wescomp too, only I'm in sales." As they sped down the freeway Jason engaged her in conversation, choosing undemanding subjects that quickly put her at ease.

"When Mr. Bradshaw asked me to escort you I thought: Oh boy, the old guy doesn't even give her credit for being able to find her own date!" he exclaimed ruefully. "But he explained how you weren't really beginning work for another week and it would be awkward for you to walk into a room full of strange people and be a conversational wizard. I guess I was chosen because I talk so much and most people don't have to worry about responding. All they have to do is nod their heads occasionally and I'm happy."

"Well, I can't complain," Dianna laughed, thinking his easygoing manner was a pleasant change from the aggressiveness of most men she'd met. "You've certainly done most of the talking so far."

He grinned sheepishly. "A less polite way of putting it would be to say I've completely monopolized the conversation!"

They laughed again and he continued to talk, finally asking the inevitable question. "Tabby's a cute little thing. Is she your niece?"

She stiffened slightly. "No, Tabby's my daughter."

"Oh, really?" he asked, surprised. "You don't look old enough to be anyone's mother. I know you don't look like my mother did when I was around Tabby's age."

"Not so long ago?" she teased, hoping to change the subject.

"Hey, I'm not that young! I'm twenty-four!" Dianna smiled at his attempt at a forbidding and dignified scowl.

They pulled into Wescomp's underground parking lot and Dianna stepped from the car, noticing the bright lights and warm colors that helped relieve the tedious stretch of gray-colored concrete. Stationed at various intervals about the well-lit garage were several uniformed security guards.

"What a good idea," Dianna murmured, nodding her head toward the nearest of the men.

Jason took her elbow and guided her toward the elevators. "It was put into practice years ago. There are too many young women working at Wescomp to chance their safety. It's rumored that a girl was raped down here once and they've had security guards ever since."

The blood slowly drained from her face and her legs trembled with an uncontrollable weakness. A deadly quiet surrounded them except for the sound of the elevator making its creaky way toward the basement. Fine dots of perspiration beaded her upper lip and forehead as her eyes darted around the concrete walls. She had never been in the garage since that night . . . never related it to . . . she had forgotten . . .

A Cadillac. Charles had driven to the dinner club in a royal blue Cadillac with seats so soft they enveloped her in a silky, spongy cocoon. It was a perfect start to what promised to be a perfect evening.

She had met Charles earlier that day when she had applied for a position with his brother's computer company. He was a young man with a permanently etched frown and caramel-colored hair. And when he smiled away the frown he was charming. She had given in to his easy banter and allowed him a date that very night to celebrate her new position.

The food was good, the wine better, and as the evening wore on she was put at ease by his bright smiles and too many sips of wine. Charles never let her glass get more than half empty. Fresh out of college and thrilled at the prospect of starting her first job, she had been too naive to heed the warning bells in her head whenever Charles gazed longingly at her. But when he held her too close as they danced around the postage-stamp floor she pushed away slightly, only to see his brow furrow a second before he smiled again. It was a funny smile, one that sent a chill down her spine for no reason at all. How could she be afraid of the young man who owned half the company for which she would be working?

"Ready to go?" His voice was slurred and Dianna wondered how many glasses of wine he had had to drink. She couldn't remember.

The radio speakers inside the Cadillac emitted slow seductive music and Dianna relaxed, leaning her head back and closing her eyes as they exited the parking lot and turned into the downtown streets. She'd declined his offer of a nightcap at the penthouse apartment he shared with his brother in the Wescomp building, but within minutes Charles had made a wide rough curve into the building's underground parking garage. He pulled the car to a short stop scant inches from the brick wall of the elevator shaft. Confused by the deliberate way he'd ignored her request to be driven home, Dianna blinked, looking at him to see eyes dilated with drink leering at her in the dashboard's dim light.

"Dianna! Mrs. Hammond! Are you all right?" Jason repeated, giving her shoulder a slight shake. She turned wide unseeing eyes up to him as slow-building panic bubbled in her throat to block off air. She was rooted to the concrete, transported into time past as its memories kept her in a viselike grip and shut out the present completely.

Charles had reached for her, pulling her close to press his lips against hers. At first, she resisted, but he paid no attention. Then she went limp, hoping he would stop when she didn't respond. His behavior was more irritating than frightening.

Suddenly he became rough and ground his mouth against hers, harder, harder, until she tasted the warm saltiness of her own blood. Only then did she push with all her might. Her mind refused to accept what he was doing. Soon he would recover and apologize. She knew it!

When his hand reached down to cruelly grab her breast and knead it painfully against arched ribs, terror washed over her. She made a superhuman effort to fight him off, but his grip didn't lessen until her elbow hit his stomach. She struggled, wrenching herself free of his grip and reaching for the door handle only to fumble in her haste. He recovered quickly and lunged at her before she could force it open, knocking her head against the unpadded edge just below the window. Stars exploded in front of her eyes and she lay dazed, hardly aware of the ripping noise her blouse made as he tore the buttons off in his fury. Her skirt was pushed up with rough hands, the panties pulled until the thin elastic ate into the tender flesh of her legs. She felt his hot breath on her breast and the coolness of the night air on her tear-stained cheeks. Her mouth kept forming words to implore him to stop, but her voice came out in a whimper.

"No!" she moaned as she tried to push him away again and again. He was angered even more and bit into the upper softness of her breast and her moans became screams. Was that her voice? Why did it sound so far away? All she knew was pain, a terrible agonizing pain that spread through her entire body.

"Shut up!" he muttered as he tried to control her swinging arms. Grabbing her shoulders, he banged her against the door again. And again. Darkness surrounded her and she wondered if she was blind. Her eyes were open, weren't they?

His fingers ruthlessly pushed between her thighs and once again a moan turned into a cry. One hand slapped her face, knocking her head sideways and hurting her cut cheek again. Salty tears streamed down her face to mingle with the blood and cause a new burning sting, but she hardly felt it.

His hands were all over her, kneading, pushing, tearing. She was lying on the seat now, no longer fighting, her mind closed to the actions in the car except to hear his cursing and the rasp of his short heavy breathing. Suddenly her limp hand came into contact with something on the floor of the car: her shoe? She grasped it by the sole, the heel free, and with the last bit of her strength, she swung it as hard as she could, aiming for his head. Her hand continued its arc even as a piercing pain lit a searing hot fire between her thighs . . .

"My God!" Then nothing.

"Mrs. Hammond!" Jason exclaimed, now worried.

Dianna's breath came in short, uneven gasps as the elevator door opened and a tall imposing figure stepped off to block her flight. She was stilled by the knowing gray-black eyes that held her, calmed her. He gave a quick glance at Jason and motioned him into the elevator as his hand reached for Dianna's. She held tightly, her knuckles white with strain as he placed her hand on his arm and turned slowly back to the opened door. She moved like an automaton as they entered the elevator and the door quietly closed.

"It's nice to see you again, Dianna. I was just coming down to greet you, remembering that you were never fond of closed-in places." His voice was low and soothing, as if he were talking to a child.

Dianna kept her eyes fixed on the floor as the relived terror slowly subsided and she realized the complete fool she had made of herself. But even as the fear receded, she could not deny the relief that flooded through her at his mere presence. He had known what to do then, just as he knew what to do now. What would she have done if he had not been there? The words of gratitude slipped out with quiet sincerity.

"Thank you, Noah."

2

~~~~~~~~~~~~~~~~

So that was it!" A relieved smile broke across Jason's face. "You gave me quite a fright down there. But I understand—I'm that way about a few things myself." His reply was tinged with humor and sympathy. "I'll bet just hearing the sound of those rusty cables echoing in the concrete basement touched it off. They really do make an eerie noise at night."

"Then we'll have to do something about that, won't we?" Noah Weston stated calmly, his dark gray hawklike eyes never leaving Dianna's face. "We can't have the new head of Programming afraid every time she . . . steps into an elevator." His voice was cool, slow, but there was another message beneath his words. Dianna understood: she couldn't relive that one night for the rest of her life. But she also knew that the terror this place held for her could never be erased. She stared up at him with a look that told him so. His smile was tinged with sardonic amusement and for a split second Dianna knew what pure and raging hatred was. She tried to wrench her hand away, but he tightened his and held her more securely. She couldn't free herself unless she wanted to make a scene. —

"Do you two know each other?" Jason asked. Before an answer could be given the elevator doors quietly opened and they stepped out.

"We've met," Noah said noncommittally as he walked her down the wide hall toward music and voices. "Would you care to freshen up, Mrs. Hammond?" he said in a low voice, emphasizing her marital status.

Fear and anger fought, and anger won. Her hazel eyes flashed, her expression looking more determined with each passing second. "Thank you. Please don't wait for me. I'll find my own way to the party," she answered stiffly.

He threw back his head and laughed, his eyes lit with amusement at her discomfort. "I doubt if you could find your way out of an empty room, but I wasn't going to wait for you. Jason will do that." He glanced over his shoulder at the puzzled younger man. "Won't you, Jason?"

Jason murmured something about never leaving a beautiful woman's side, but Dianna was too angry to pay attention. She made her way across the carpeted hall to the ladies' room and walked in, closing the door softly with the last of her control.

She never should have come! Tears pushed at her eyelids and she had a hard time preventing them from coursing down her cheeks. The shaking in her limbs made her sit on the dressing-table stool, taking deep breaths of air, trying to reason herself into composure.

Noah would never mention what had happened seven years ago—his family's reputation was at stake, and that alone would keep him quiet. Why would he want to say anything anyway? After all, he didn't know about Tabby! Dianna took another deep breath. She had been running from shadows again. She would go back out and face him, knowing there was no harm he could do to her. Then all would be back to normal. Yes, that was it. All she had to do was act cool and composed, never allowing him to see the state her nerves were in. Once this party was over she probably wouldn't see the president of Wescomp more than a few times a year.

She hoped her casual exterior wouldn't crack as she left the lounge and walked toward Jason, ignoring the tall arrogant man who stood in the doorway of the reception room watching her intently with a small secret smile on his lips. The smile she aimed at Jason was more brilliant than she intended and his eyes lit up in appreciation.

"I always said there was something about an older woman that brought out the best in me," he teased as he took her arm and they began walking toward the noisy gathering.

"Something along the lines of a mother figure?"

"Ouch, lady!"

She gave his arm a squeeze, more from nerves than friendliness. They were approaching Noah and she needed to repeat her silent pep talk. "Just teasing. Sorry. I can tell the difference between a man and a boy." She spoke absently, not knowing how provocative her words sounded.

"Yes, but Jason hasn't learned the difference between a witty woman and a shrew." Noah's voice intruded on their banter, soft and lazy with just a hint of sarcasm. "Watch it, Jason. She might decide to eat you for breakfast." His grin was maddening. He was playing cat and mouse with her, and she wasn't the one wearing the Cheshire smile!

Her face was mockingly innocent. "I thought that's what you did!"

"I gave you my answer to that long ago, Mrs. Hammond. But times have changed and people have aged. What was young then is older and more experienced now." His voice held the hint of a threat, but Jason didn't pick it up.

"And what was tender then is no longer. You might find the meal tough and not at all to your liking," she replied coolly.

"That's true, but I always did like a challenge."

"Not this one," she murmured sweetly, not showing a hint of displeasure. She tried to pass him in the doorway, but he stood complacently blocking her entrance.

Jason halted, watching both of them with a puzzled expression, trying to understand the thrust-and-parry conversation. There was more to it than was immediately apparent, but he couldn't get below the surface. His face showed his confusion as he took Dianna's arm possessively, nodding his head toward the back of the room.

"I see Miss Sinclair is here. She's very beautiful tonight, as usual." Jason's voice was louder than normal, attracting the attention of a stunningly lovely woman who stood on the other side of the room. She walked toward them with a feline grace; her blond hair flowed about her shoulders, framing beautifully sculpted features and wide blue eyes. Her pale blue dress, a designer original, showed off an enticingly voluptuous figure. She came to Noah's side and slipped a proprietorial arm in his.

"Darling, I was wondering where you were. You left me all alone to cope with this crowd," she complained, her bright cherry lips pouting flirtatiously.

"I'm sure you did very well, Kitty. I notice you weren't shy of male company—half the board of directors was paying court." He grinned, the cleft in his chin deepening.

"Half your board is over fifty and balding!"

"But that didn't stop you from basking in the limelight." Noah glanced around the room as if only a portion of his attention was on their conversation. Then he remembered the present company and turned to introduce them.

"Kitty, I'd like you to meet Mrs. Hammond and Jason Manners. This is Catherine Sinclair, a very talented young country-and-Western singer. I'm backing her to go far in the music world."

Catherine's eyes narrowed on Dianna before she shrugged her shoulders in dismissal and turned a charming smile on Jason.

"You were at the Greer party, weren't you?"

"I didn't think you'd remember." Jason grinned uneasily, glancing quickly at Noah.

"I wasn't that drunk, darling. Though Noah deserves to find me in that shape if he tries to make a habit out of going to parties just to discuss business and leaves me on my own."

"Enough, Catherine. I doubt if my employees are

concerned with your vices." A muscle in the side of his jaw was tightened in disapproval. There was still a ruthless quality about him that reached out and touched Dianna, sending warning signals through her body. Never underestimate him, she told herself. Never underestimate the devil.

"But, darling, surely my vices matter very little to Wescomp compared to yours!"

"And neither is up for discussion," he stated grimly. "If you want to join the party I suggest you behave yourself, now, or you'll lead me to think that you should be on your way home—alone."

Noah's last comment hit home, and Catherine's face showed the sting of his words. His threat had effectively silenced her. Dianna stood quietly, not realizing how tightly she had been clutching Jason's arm until Noah noticed it, then looked at her, his deep gray eyes seeming to read her very thoughts. He stepped aside, murmuring to Jason to be sure to introduce Dianna to all and sundry, and dismissed them.

Jason escorted her toward the milling group around the long hors-d'oeuvre table. An ice sculpture of a large robot stood in the center of the table, the accuracy and intricacy of design making it a work of art.

They began circulating from group to group, names tumbling over names as Dianna smiled prettily, becoming further withdrawn at the strangeness of it all. These were the elite of Dallas, known to her only from the newspaper columns. First, she felt awed, then charmed. Only occasionally did the men show their feet of clay and the women their boredom and unhappiness. They were all striving to maintain the image of the beautiful people, even among themselves.

She recognized some of the many prominent guests as her glance darted around the large room. Judge Hawthorne was talking to the new young Senator Greer and a few others. The senator's light brown hair and eyes and his smooth boyish face were easily recognizable. Dianna vaguely remembered reading an article concerning his future plans to run for the Presidency.

His wife stood in a darkened corner of the room, her head leaning on a stocky older man's shoulder, arms entwined in his. He had been pointed out earlier as a famous character actor. Although his face was familiar, Dianna couldn't remember his name. Mrs. Greer was obviously tipsy and in the mood for making love, but not with her boy-child husband. Her husky laughter floated across the room and Dianna watched the senator give a cursory glance in her direction before scanning the crowd. His eyes locked with Dianna's and after his apparent surprise at a new and lovely face, he smiled. Dianna returned his smile, giving a slight negative shake of her head to his unspoken question. He registered disappointment before turning to prowl the rest of the room.

Jason's arm went lightly around her waist as he turned to introduce her to Thomas Beloit, a man that Jason apparently held in awe, at least judging by the tone of his voice. He had been highlighted in the Texas magazines off and on, escorting one starlet or another. He still held much charm, although late nights and heavy drinking had taken their toll. When they were introduced his eyes lit with interest before his lids drooped to disguise his thoughts.

"And you honestly work for Noah? He isn't as quick to notice a beautiful woman as I once thought. My only hope is to get to know you before he discovers your charming attributes himself, my dear." His eyes locked with hers before traveling down the length of her body, a slow smile giving his thoughts away.

"I do recognize her attributes, but I wish you would leave my employees alone, or they might get the wrong idea, Tom." Noah's voice, directly behind Dianna, seemed to come out of nowhere. She tried to ignore him, but she couldn't ignore the tingle his soft breath sent down her spine, nor could she move either forward or backward.

"If you are really interested," Noah continued, "you'll have to make plans *after* office hours."

"But this is after office hours, Noah," Tom answered silkily, his eyes never leaving Dianna's face.

"This lady doesn't belong to anyone after hours," Dianna interjected, "so I'd appreciate not being handed from one to another of you like a sheaf of papers." She forced herself to smile the words, then sipped on her cocktail to quiet the rest of her thoughts. She didn't see Noah's admiration at the flame of temper that lit up her large hazel eyes, nor did she realize that anger had given a glow to her usually pale skin. All she could do was pretend to be composed. She was totally conscious of Noah's lean length directly behind her, making her feel that they were in intimate contact though their bodies never touched. Even his breath caressed her, frightening her with the reaction it produced on her heightened senses.

She turned quickly to Jason, linking her arm in his as she assumed a light note. "How about getting something to eat, Jason?"

"Delighted," Jason answered smoothly as he led her

away from both men and into calmer waters, glad for once to be around to see the big boys receive a set-down.

Later, as they helped themselves to an array of delicacies, Jason introduced her to a few more people. The group on their right consisted of a publishing agent, a movie star's somewhat disenchanted husband, and a banker. She had to smile at the incongruity of them in their small circle discussing the finer points of tennis as if they had known each other for years.

She and Jason made small talk while one part of her tired mind attempted to blot out Noah's presence. She shouldn't have come. The episode in the basement was only a part of the reason for her tense muscles. Her hands trembled as if she had a chill, and no matter how many times she told herself to relax, the feeling of impending doom would not go away. Why was it she was capable of handling all the men in the room . . . except Noah?

She watched the young senator amble over to a blonde in a tight-fitting red jersey dress and wondered who she had come with. Dianna had seen her with another man earlier.

"So this is society," she murmured to herself as she bit into a small sausage roll.

"This is it. But don't judge them too harshly, Dianna. They work hard and play hard. It's my guess that money hasn't bought them any real happiness." Jason looked sad as his eyes scanned the room before resting on Dianna's downbent head.

"I can't judge them. I just don't want to watch them condemn themselves."

"You're as white as a sheet. Let's sit down and relax." He reached out to take a champagne cocktail from a passing waiter, then walked her to an unoccupied seat away from the pressing crowd.

Dianna sat down, giving a grateful smile to her partner.

"This is much better, don't you agree?" Jason asked as he leaned back, balancing his drink on his thigh. "What do you think of your new boss? Not quite the run of the mill, is he?"

"Run of the mill?" Dianna repeated guardedly. She had already had too much contact with Noah Weston for her taste. There was something about the man that was too imposing, too . . . masculine. But if it meant the difference between Tabby well and Tabby ill, then there was no choice. No choice at all.

Jason gave her a look she couldn't quite read. "A guy who has everything—success, good looks, money, power—and all before he's forty. That's a rare man these days." He smiled his little-boy smile. "He's quite a guy. Especially with the girls, or haven't you noticed?"

Dianna knew exactly what he was asking, and she had to smile at his transparency. He was as easy to read as Tabby!

"Since I'm no longer a girl, I guess I'm immune. Besides, there's his obvious arrangement with Catherine Sinclair."

Jason had the grace to look slightly sheepish. "This seems to be my night for being caught just outside the orchard with stolen apples," he answered ruefully. "But I don't think Catherine the Great has him as sewn up as the public thinks. If she did, then they'd be married by now."

"What makes you say that?"

"Two things. One, she's been in his little black book for over a year, and he hasn't seen fit to take her home to meet his sister. Two, Mr. Weston has money in a record company and she's the big singing star, so I think he's trying to keep her happy until her contract is over. At any rate, I think he's just playing her along until something better comes his way. He doesn't seem the sort to let a woman he's really interested in get away with the things she does."

"He lives with his sister?" Dianna asked, surprised. He'd never mentioned the existence of a sister when she'd known him!

"Yes, or at least she lives on his ranch. She's much older than he is and raised him after their parents died. They had a younger brother, but he was killed in an auto accident several years ago. Right after that she had a stroke, and he's taken care of her ever since."

"I didn't know," she whispered, her face turning pale under the dim lighting of the room. *Charles was dead!* The words echoed in her mind, but she couldn't seem to believe them. She sipped on her cocktail and stared straight ahead, not wanting to make conversation. She just wanted to leave, go home to Tabby. But she couldn't.

Her eyes sought Noah, watching him as he moved from group to group. He looked so distinguished in a tuxedo. His sideburns, lightly flecked with premature gray, accented the dark handsome features of a man obviously in charge. His hair was almost as black as Dianna's. His skin, a coppery color, told of a great deal of time spent outdoors. Dark brows slashed straight across his arrogant Roman nose. His jaw was square; a deep cleft in the center of his bottom lip softened the look of determination that marked his appearance. His smile was devastating and he seemed to listen with honest interest to every conversation. What sort of man was he? He was considerate of other people, yet he seemed cruel in his relationship with Catherine. Which was the act and which the real Noah? She listened vaguely to the nonsense conversation Jason was holding with the older woman on his other side, but when he turned to include her she was so startled she jumped.

"Hey, I didn't mean to scare you!" he exclaimed. "Are you feeling all right?" His honest concern was almost too much for Dianna. The composure that had taken her years to build up was slipping away in one night. "Would you like to leave? This is almost over anyway."

She nodded her head, relieved at his suggestion. Her hazel eyes shimmered to an emerald green with unshed tears.

"Let's go." He stood and took her arm, leading her toward the far door. Just as they reached it a tall figure blocked their way.

"Leaving so soon, Mrs. Hammond?" Noah asked, one black brow raised slightly, showing just a hint of boredom, as if he were asking more out of politeness than concern.

"I think Mrs. Hammond is worried about her daughter," Jason replied quickly, defending her with the one piece of information she had not wanted uttered. She shook her head, denying his excuse.

"I'm sorry, Mr. Weston, but I'm just not used to parties. I've acquired a terrible headache," she murmured, knowing it to be the truth. Her head was throbbing heavily, in time with her pulsebeat, and there was a definite hot spot behind her eyes. Tension had taken its toll and she knew the symptoms well enough to know she had to sleep the headache off.

"I'll take Mrs. Hammond home, Jason," Noah decided abruptly, ignoring the young man's surprised stare. "You stay and help Miss Sinclair enjoy the party. It's almost over anyway." He turned to Catherine, who had come to stand at his side with an expression of barely concealed impatience. She gave Noah a coy glance and tucked her arm possessively in his.

"Really, Noah. I'm sure Jason doesn't mind driving Mrs. Hammond home." She smiled sweetly, but the emphasis on "Mrs." was not lost, and Dianna's face turned pink as she met Catherine's cold eyes.

Dianna swallowed hard. There had to be a way to get out of this impossible situation! "Please," she said quietly and with as much dignity as her tattered nerves would allow. "I'll get a taxi. I'm sure there are plenty around." She turned to Jason and held out her hand. "Thank you, Jason. It was a pleasure meeting you." She smiled thinly. "Good night, all."

She walked quickly out the door and down the wide corridor toward the elevators. Her legs were curiously weak as she waited for the doors to open and swallow her. Her head was spinning and she placed a hand on the cool metal door to steady herself. Just at that moment the doors silently slid open, almost knocking her off balance. A pair of strong arms came around her, guiding her inside the elevator, and the doors closed silently behind them. The elevator was moving by the time she turned to confront her rescuer.

"Thank you, but I can make it the rest of the way by myself." She spoke more curtly than she had intended, but would not relent as she stared into his gray-black eyes.

"I don't remember asking you," he retorted, his usually sensuous lips pressed together in an uncompromising line, emphasizing his irritation.

Tension crackled in the air as their eyes locked and fought a silent battle of wills, but Dianna lowered her lashes just as the elevator stopped and the doors opened. Instead of the expected view of the lobby, she was met by the sight of an all-too-familiar hallway—the hallway outside Noah Weston's penthouse suite. A man in a guard uniform stood leaning against the wall, a magazine in his hand. When he spotted them he straightened, watching Noah guide her toward the apartment door.

"Evening, Simon," Noah muttered.

"Good evening, sir." The man smiled, his expression both respectful and curious. Dianna wanted to turn and run, but the pressure of Noah's hand prevented her retreat more effectively than locks or keys could. The door opened to his touch and he led the way down the small narrow hallway to the large living room. It was all just as she remembered it: the glass wall overlooking the city, the expensive furnishings, the quietly elegant tan-and-brown color scheme. Gently he pushed her into a chair and leaned over, holding Dianna hostage as his hands gripped the sides of the cushioned arms.

"Sit here and keep quiet for a minute," he ordered before walking to a paneled wall and touching a small brown button. The wall rotated, disclosing a completely mirrored bar that revolved into the room to display fine cut crystal of every shape and size. Bottles of expensive liqueurs were standing on the back shelf. He poured a pure white liquid into two small stemmed glasses and returned to stand in front of her, staring down as if not really seeing her at all. He thrust the drink into her trembling hand.

"This will help your headache." He turned, then sat heavily in the chair across from hers. Dianna sipped it, barely noticing its licorice taste or the soothing way it passed down her dry throat. Dianna's eyes were focused on Noah.

"Why did you run away, all those years ago?" he asked abruptly.

"I should think that was obvious," she retorted with more bravado than she felt. "What did you expect me to do, remain here indefinitely?"

"I expected you to know that I would take care of you."

"What I didn't need was your care, pity, or charity!" The walls began closing in around her. She couldn't breathe. Why did he affect her like this? After what had happened in the past she should be immune to him. If she could just leave, then everything would be all right. Everything would be fine.

"I never wanted to give you pity or charity, just care, in the form of a home and a reasonable income for the rest of your life."

"For services rendered?" she sneered. "No thanks! I've managed on my own for all these years, so please don't start worrying about me now. If that's the reason your company accepted my application, then you can take your position, your reasonable income, and whatever else your 'company benefits' are and stick them in your ear!" she exclaimed, standing quickly.

"Sit down before you fall down!" he gritted. "I'm not through with you yet!"

She sank into the chair slowly, watching him as he refilled his glass at the bar. She was tuned to his anger, his thoughts. She knew what he was going to ask next, and she didn't want to answer. Suddenly all the fight went out of her, but determination remained. She stared down at her hands like a gypsy looking into a crystal ball.

"Tell me about your daughter." He stood towering over her, blocking any escape she might have made.

"There's nothing to tell," she said slowly, knowing she had to be on guard against this man and the power any information concerning Tabby could give him.

"I'll be the judge of that," he retorted impatiently. "What's her name? How old is she?"

"Her name is Tabby, short for Tabitha. She's six years old."

"Six," he mused as if to himself. "And who do you claim is the father?" His eyes locked with hers. This questioning was not a whim, but a deliberate searching for the truth—a truth she would not supply. She struggled for the words she needed to disarm him.

"Her father was a man I met right after . . . after that week. He died shortly after we were married." Her voice was steady, as was her gaze.

"And he had the same last name as yours?"

"Yes."

"Do you expect me to believe this?"

"Believe what you want." She rose to her feet, disregarding the thousands of butterflies beating against the lining of her stomach. Unconsciously she placed one hand on the side of her throbbing head.

He watched her movements through narrowed eyes, without speaking. The silence roared in Dianna's ears.

"Just one more thing, Dianna. Why did you decide to

apply for a job at Wescomp? I'm curious, since it obviously wasn't my winning personality you wanted to be near."

"Because the money is better than I've been receiving, and the opportunity for advancement is greater."

"Any other reasons I should know about?" His body was almost touching hers, sending heat waves to surround and suffocate her. He was not going to let her pass.

"One other reason, yes." She swayed slightly and Noah brought his hands up to her waist, holding her steady. "You have an excellent medical plan and Tabby has a health problem."

"What kind of health problem?" His voice was low, husky, more like a caress than a question. But he was still watching her like a waiting panther debating if it had a full stomach or room enough to digest one more morsel.

"She has a small hole in the wall of her heart that will need expensive surgery to correct." She turned her head away from his eyes, her senses reeling at his touch, but she couldn't move. "Surely none of this has to do with my qualifications, Mr. Weston?"

"Qualifications? No, it has nothing to do with your job at Wescomp." His hands were moving from her waist to her back, and she stared at him, looking more vulnerable than she knew. His gaze searched her face intently, seeing the tension and pain she tried so hard to hide.

"I just don't like secrets, Mrs. Hammond, and you're the secretive kind."

"Everyone has . . ." She hesitated.

He broke in, a stern look on his face, his jaw clenched. "Skeletons in the closet?"

"Something like that, yes."

"But your skeleton is so interesting," he mocked.

Her voice was cold as she spoke, belying the fear in her eyes. "But it is *my* skeleton!"

"Are you sure you didn't return to Wescomp to ask for help with . . . your daughter?" he asked softly, one mocking brow raised, his eyes narrowed.

"If you think that, then you're way off the mark! I'm an expert in my field. I applied for the job because I thought I could give my skill for an equally good salary. If you didn't want me, you should have taken care to have my application turned down!" she hissed. "Or is it your ego talking? Do you think *every* female is out to get you?"

"They usually are."

"You insufferable, conceited . . ."

His hands tightened warningly. "Watch it, or I may take you up on your offer of resignation. Then where would Tabby be?" Noah didn't bother to hide the sarcasm in his tone. His eyes glittered dangerously.

She slumped visibly. Somehow, with a minimum of questioning, he had discovered her Achilles' heel. She knew he would use it.

"Let me go." A coldness enveloped her as his arms dropped and he stepped away, his face a mask.

"Gladly."

Her head began spinning, her hands were clammy with sweat. She felt herself falling and reached for the table, but it wasn't there. Bile rose in her throat, only to back down again. In the next second she was in Noah's strong arms, being carried into a darkened room. The absence of light made the throbbing pain behind her eyes subside slightly.

"I'm sorry," she murmured, "but my head . . ."

"You suffer from migraine?"

"Yes, but I haven't had one in such a long time. I haven't . . ."

He laid her down carefully. The coolness of the satin coverlet felt good against her heated skin. His arms slipped away but his voice was close to her ear as he spoke.

"Lie still. I'll be back in a minute." His footsteps were muffled on the thick carpeting as he left the room. She could hear him speaking to someone on the phone, then a light was flicked on in the connecting bath. She shrank from the glare, hiding her head in the soft pillow. The light disappeared and a cool cloth was placed on her forehead.

"Rest," she heard Noah's voice whisper, and she gave a sigh.

His hands were gentle as he stroked her temples, brushing back a few stray wisps of hair, soothing her, stroking her into a deep relaxation.

She had done it. She had kept her secret. She had bearded the lion in his den and come out unscathed. Almost.

3

June stood by the living-room window as she watched Noah step out of his sleek midnight-blue Mercedes. Her stomach cramped into a tight ball—even tighter than when Noah had called last night. Was he telling the truth? Had Dianna really decided he should meet Tabby? If that was so, then why wasn't Dianna here to help with the introductions between the child and her uncle? Was she really ill, or was that just an excuse on Noah's part? June ignored the small frightened voice that echoed in her head, telling her she was believing Noah because she had no choice, no choice at all.

David answered the door and led Noah into the living room, making polite introductions that were not needed. June poured coffee with slightly shaking hands and listened to the two men discuss Tabby's future impersonally, as if she were a stock in which they were interested in investing. She knew she was the only one with misgivings, because David's eyes were bright with unashamed envy and Noah's lit with interest at every bit of information about Tabby's life to date. Noah spoke vaguely of his future plans for Tabby and Dianna, and June wondered if even he knew what he was going to do next. She pushed the thought away quickly. He was too decisive a man *not* to have some plan already worked out. Her only worry was whether he would help or hinder Dianna. But she couldn't voice her thoughts to either of these men. They both thought they knew best. She was only there as silent proxy for her sister.

"June." Noah's voice broke into her troubled thoughts and she sat straighter in her chair, much like a young girl in a principal's office. "How much of Dianna's story is made up? She informed Mr. Bradshaw that she had been married. Is that true?"

"Of course not!" June spouted indignantly. Noah of all people should have known that. "Dianna told everyone she was married to hide the fact that she was having a child out of wedlock—the story was used for protection. We all know Tabby is Charles's child."

"Really? And what makes you so sure?" He crossed his legs and leaned back in the chair, but June wasn't fooled. She knew he would pounce on her in a moment if he thought she wasn't telling the truth.

"Because Dianna never dated. Two years ago she was

escorted to several parties that her company asked her to attend. But until then she had not dated anyone for five years!"

"Not even directly after the rape?"

June winced at his words, but her eyes locked with his. She could be just as stubborn as he! "*Especially* after that! She didn't leave this house for over six months. Not even to travel to the store alone. All she did was sit alone in her room and stare out at the backyard," June said emphatically. "If you're trying to prove that Charles was not Tabby's father, you can forget it." She took a deep breath and plunged. "You should have been here after that . . . that night. You should have helped Dianna with Tabby long ago when she needed all the moral support she could get. Tabby is definitely a Weston, and Charles is to blame. We all know that." She looked toward David for reinforcement, which he gave in the form of an affirmative nod.

"*I* know who's to blame, but apparently no one else does," Noah said cryptically, then gave an apologetic sigh. "All right. If we're to say I'm Tabby's uncle, then we'll leave it that way . . . for now."

"But it's true!" June looked from Noah's disbelieving face to the puzzled expression of her husband. "Double check with that private detective you sent around right after Dianna applied for the job with Wescomp. He probably interviewed half the neighborhood!" The bitterness that laced her words was obvious to both men, but as Noah started to speak a small voice broke the silence.

"Are you Mr. Weston?" Tabby asked as she stood in the doorway of the living room and stared at the tall stranger seated in Aunt June's best chair. "Are you really my uncle?"

Noah's mouth moved into a smile that lit up his gray eyes. "I'm really your uncle, and I've come to meet you. I heard you were a beautiful young lady and I wanted to see for myself whether it was true."

Her hazel eyes stared at him before she answered. It was as if she were not listening to him, but to some voice deep inside that weighed the truth of his words. Slowly her smile grew. She stepped into the room, stopping just short of Noah's chair. "You must have talked to my mother. She always says I'm beautiful."

"And she's right."

"I want to look just like her when I grow up. An' I will too," she stated, holding on to one long corn-colored pigtail, "'cept for my hair."

Noah swallowed a lump in his throat before answering. "I think you look just like her now," he answered softly. "Except for the hair. That comes from your father's side of the family. All the Westons have hair your color when they're young. Some keep it and others grow darker, as I did."

"You had my color hair?"

"Once, when I was a little boy, just about your age."

"Are you very old now?" She tilted her head to one side and studied the smile lines around his eyes very carefully.

"Tabby! That's not polite, dear," June admonished, but Noah's hand rose to halt her speech, his eyes never leaving Tabby.

"Not too old yet, Tabby. How old are you?"

"I'll be seven in March." She stood just a little taller, proud of her claim to years. Suddenly a cloud passed over her face and she looked uncertainly at her aunt, then back to Noah. "Aunt June says my mom doesn't feel well. She says you're taking care of her. Is that right?"

"Your mother feels better already, Tabby. I just thought she needed rest. Do you mind not seeing her for a few days? Your aunt has offered to have you stay here and play with your cousins. That way your mother won't worry about all the things that need to be done and get tired again."

"I don't mind as long as she gets better. I'm all she has, you see." Her lower lip trembled slightly and Noah unconsciously put his hand over her small one, surprised at the frailty of her tiny bones.

From the moment Tabby had entered the room all cynicism had fled his features and June had glimpsed another facet of his character. But now, even laughter was erased as he returned her serious look.

"I know. I'd like to help you take care of your mother so she doesn't get so tired again. Do you think we could take a drive and talk about it?"

Before June knew what had happened, Tabby and Noah were gone, promising to return in an hour. Everything was out of her hands now and there was nothing else she could do. Noah had neatly maneuvered her by playing on her own feelings that justice should be done. "Dear God, let this work out," she prayed as she absently straightened the cushions on the couch. "Please let this work out!"

As promised, Noah had Tabby back inside the security of June's house within the hour. He spoke with June and David again, giving a few more details of his plans for the woman and child he had taken into his protection, then bid Tabby an affectionate farewell, once more swallowing the lump that formed every time he looked at her.

Five minutes later he was entering the flow of traffic on the freeway back to town. Reflexes took over the driving as his mind wrapped around a jumble of thoughts. There was so little the private detective had been able to tell him over the past few weeks. He hadn't mentioned how thin the child was, or how sweet. He never said how grown up she behaved as she pondered questions before putting an answer to them. Tabby was a Weston, all right. Any doubts he might have harbored had been blown to bits the minute he saw her standing in the doorway. Dianna had to be given credit for raising her to be such a charming little girl. She had done her job well. And without his help.

He turned the wheel slightly to adjust to the curve of the highway. Now all he had to do was clear Catherine out of the way and Tabby could step into her rightful place, along with her mother. But that wasn't going to be easy.

He had first met Catherine Sinclair three years ago in Nashville at a run-down recording studio his friend and lawyer Philip Young had assured him was a sound investment. The nineteen-year-old girl had shown promise and he had made sure she got the break she was looking for. The rest she had done herself.

She'd soon made a good-sized splash in country-and-Western circles and before long had cut two gold records. Then, last year while on tour, she'd made a surprise visit to Dallas to thank her benefactor, she said. She had changed from the cheeky, scrappy kid he had first met into a sophisticated young woman with the sensuousness of a she-cat. It was obvious from the first that she had more than gratitude in mind, and he hadn't objected. They both understood the nature of their relationship, or so he had thought. Only lately had he realized just how much she'd begun to expect of him. He had used her, true, but she was out to use him to far greater advantage.

The strings would be cut. Noah would give her the piece of jewelry she had been hinting for and show her the door. It was the least he could do. She had been there when he needed her on dark lonely nights. It didn't matter that any female would have satisfied that part of him: she had been there, never asking questions when he performed separate from his thoughts. She had never asked for more than physical release; and Noah, haunted by an image from the past—a vision of silky skin, dark flowing hair, and bright hazel eyes—could never give more than that. Perhaps she had known.

He pulled into the underground garage, parking his car next to the elevator and stepping out. First things first— right now his problem was Dianna.

Consciousness came too soon. Dianna suffered a thick tongue, a dull throb at the base of her neck, and a weighted, lifeless body. It took all her strength to move reluctant legs to a more comfortable position. She knew she was feeling the aftereffects of the shot administered by the doctor last night. She vaguely remembered bits and pieces of the conversation, but the pain had been too intense for her to concentrate on anything.

She forced her eyes open and slowly looked around the familiar surroundings. The room was just as it had been seven years ago, decorated in shades of chocolate and rust and almost overwhelmingly masculine. The furniture was all in natural wood, polished to a high mirrorlike gloss. The king-size bed sat upon a carpeted dais, and the bedspread was a patchwork of earth tones in a geometric design. Noah's forceful personality was stamped on everything. He had good taste. He always had.

Noah. He was a puzzle in the shape of a man. Last night he had taunted, teased, cajoled, threatened. Then, when he realized she was truly ill and her nerves were stretched to the breaking point, he had been tender. He had bathed her forehead, called the doctor, then cradled her gently in the darkened room. He had been ruthless but he'd proved he could also be gentle. The doctor had come and gone quickly, allowing Dianna to surrender to the dark curtain that wrapped her in black, blessed peace. But just before she was captured by oblivion Noah had whispered a question, and she had answered truthfully. What was the question? Was Tabby a Weston? Yes.

She sat upright. An explosion in her head sent bolts of lightning heat through her body as she realized the consequences of her honesty. He knew! Damn him! He had tricked her into admitting what previously he could only have suspected!

She quickly scanned the room for her clothing, ignoring the heavy throbbing of her head. She had to leave. She had to pick up Tabby and leave Dallas quickly. Where would she go? Never mind, she would think of that later. It didn't really matter where they lived as long as it was far away from Noah Weston!

Panic made her slip into her dress and fumble with the zipper. She began searching the floor for her shoes. They had to be around somewhere! Then she remembered.

They had dropped off her feet last night as Noah carried her through the hallway. If she could just find them and leave quickly without seeing him! Perhaps he was still asleep? Dianna glanced at her watch and stifled a groan. It was two thirty in the afternoon. She had slept over sixteen hours!

Her heart continued to thump heavily with the strain of active movement so soon after her drug-induced sleep. She reached for her purse on the top of the dresser, only to turn and find Noah standing in the open doorway. He leaned against the door jamb with lazy indolence, an almost tangible male virility emanating from him. Her shoes dangled from his fingertips. His smile was mocking as he glanced around the room before focusing on her. "Good afternoon. Feeling better?"

"Much better, thank you." Dianna wet dry lips with the tip of her tongue. "I'm sorry for putting you out last night. I should have gone home immediately—then I wouldn't have been such a trial." She gave a shaky laugh, glancing at him through thick lashes. "I'm glad I don't have migraines often. I get into a terrible stew and say the silliest things!" She waited for him to answer . . . move, shout—anything. But he just smiled enigmatically as he watched her run a comb through her dark tangled hair. When she felt as though her nerves would snap from the strain, Noah pushed away from the door and casually walked toward her.

"Think nothing of it. I've never felt that sharing a bed with a beautiful woman was a hardship."

Her thoughts tumbled in confusion. "Share . . . ?" Dianna tried to read the answer in his eyes before staring over her shoulder to the bed. The fluffy pillows held definite imprints of two heads, and the sheets and coverlet showed signs of being disturbed on both sides.

Confusion turned to disbelief, then to humiliation as the evidence was confirmed on Noah's face. Dianna pivoted and walked to the window, turning her face from his view to keep the tears from showing. She stared unseeingly at the patio beyond.

"Dianna." He spoke softly, the teasing gone from his voice now. "The bed was all we shared. I haven't begun taking advantage of unconscious women yet. You were so drugged I didn't think you'd care where I slept. I'm sorry if I've upset you." He moved to stand directly behind her, his voice low and apologetic. "Don't you want to call Tabby and reassure her you're all right?"

"No! I'll explain when I get home." She had forgotten completely about Tabby and June. They would be worried sick, but there was no amount of worry that would make her use Noah's phone for an explanation that would be as painful and detailed as this one.

"Do you spend the night out often then?"

She turned to face him, anger taking the place of humiliation. "Yes, often."

"Liar," he said softly, amusement invading his deep voice.

"Believe what you want."

His gaze became thoughtful as he stared into large hazel eyes that held a mixture of defeat and spirit.

"They say a woman raped often becomes either a whore or a nun."

"They also say that rapists run in the family."

He ignored her sharp tongue. "I'd say that since you left me, you've played the part of a nun."

"It goes to show that even little tin gods can make mistakes," Dianna replied sweetly, but her eyes sparked fire.

"Little tin gods are better than no gods at all." He grinned. He was enjoying this! Closing the small gap between them with another step, Noah backed her toward the window and grabbed her arms. Her body stiffened but she continued to stare haughtily.

"Thank you for those words of wisdom, Mr. Weston. And now, if you'll excuse me, I'd like to throw your hospitality in your face a second time and get out of here," she mocked. Buried memories returned to make the color rise like flags on her cheeks. His eyes told her he knew her intimate thoughts and she warmed even more.

"Let go!"

"Not yet. You might like to know I saw your sister this morning and explained the situation. She was very considerate of my feelings and thanked me profusely for taking care of you. She expects you to call her later."

"You . . . you had no right!" she sputtered.

"I had every right, Dianna, and there's more to come." His grip lessened but she was held in place by his controlled anger.

"Now, stop acting like a child and finish getting dressed. I'll discuss the rest with you after lunch. It'll be served in five minutes. I expect you to join me." He turned and left the room.

Dianna stood unmoving. He knew about Tabby, and June. He apparently knew everything. What would happen next? What did he want from her? She felt drained and unable to cope with the thoughts that tried to push their way forward to be acknowledged. Right now she would take one hour at a time. Soon the whole nightmare would be over and she'd know what to do then.

Dianna splashed water on her face and applied a little makeup before leaving the room and walking down the small hallway to the dining room. It was in an L-shaped alcove just off the living area and was done in the same contemporary style as the rest of the penthouse. Noah sat at the head of the rectangular glass-topped table reading from a stack of mail at the side of his plate. A large white soup tureen sat in the center, with a basket of French bread, hot and buttered, on a small silver tray. She took the seat to his right and waited for his attention.

He glanced over several papers before looking up, a slight frown on his brow.

"Are you going to eat or sit there and stare at me?" he demanded.

"I thought I'd wait for you before I served myself."

Exasperation edged his voice. "All right, let's eat then."

"Can we talk first?"

"No. There's plenty of time for that later."

Dianna silently served up a bowl of thick beef stew, the tantalizing aroma making her suddenly aware of how hungry she was. After having served them both, she tore off a small hunk of the steaming bread and spread creamy butter over its broken edge. It tasted as good as it looked.

"Everything all right, Mr. Weston?" A middle-aged woman with a topknot of wiry gray hair and sharp gray eyes opened the swinging kitchen door, her eyebrows raised in question.

"Very good, Mrs. Frank. You've outdone yourself again." He grinned disarmingly and the older woman

55

beamed back. "Mrs. Hammond hasn't been able to say a word, she's been so busy sampling your efforts."

"Well, that's the way it should be. Good cooking deserves good appetites, and she looks like she could do with some good cooking. A mite on the thin side, I'd say." Her sharp gray eyes glanced over Dianna's form, drawing their own conclusions. "Should have her fattened up in no time!" Mrs. Frank nodded to emphasize her plan.

"I'm not a goose!" Dianna protested, torn between indignation and laughter.

"Should say not! Mr. Weston don't go for silly gooses!" she retorted, quickly shutting the door behind her large form as she disappeared into the kitchen.

Noah's eyes locked with Dianna's and grins spread across both faces before they broke into shared laughter. For an instant it was as it had been seven years ago; then the intimate moment was shattered by the overwhelming fear of the present. The rest of the meal passed in silence and when they were finished eating, Noah led the way into the living room for their coffee.

Seating himself on the leather couch, Noah reached in his pocket and produced a lighter and cigarettes. He offered one to Dianna and she accepted warily, sinking down on the cushion beside him.

"June gave me the name of Tabby's doctor and I called him this morning," Noah began without preamble. "He tells me he can operate next Friday. He doesn't think there is any time for delay. The longer he waits, the weaker Tabby becomes. In fact, if an operating room can be reserved earlier, he's taking it."

"You called Dr. Storn?"

"Yes."

"But why?"

"I take care of my own, Dianna. And Tabby belongs to me."

"No! Tabby is mine. I'm the one who raised her! I'm the one who carried her for nine months, nourished her, worried about her, took care of her! Not you! Not the formidable Westons!" She stood on shaking legs, placing the coffee cup she held on the low table before her with trembling hands.

"And you'll still be the one who cares for her. I'm just making sure Tabby will be here for both of us to enjoy later." His voice was even, but his gray-black eyes narrowed, watching reactions flit across her expressive face as if judging and weighing the best way to convince her.

"Why are you doing this?" She flung her hands out beseechingly. "You don't even know Tabby! Why are you suddenly taking such an interest in her?"

"I know more than you guess, Dianna," he returned with a mysterious look. "I met Tabby this morning while you were sleeping. You've done a wonderful job raising her, giving her a sense of belonging. I want to make sure you can continue to give her the love and stability she needs to mature into what she promises to be. Is that so wrong?"

"You saw her today?"

"Yes, today. And I might add that the rest of your family doesn't seem to regard me as a dragon." His husky voice was dry with sarcasm. "You'd think I was asking you to live in sin when all I'm doing is insuring your and Tabby's future."

"You won't take her away from me?" she asked hoarsely, afraid to find relief in his answer.

"On the contrary. I want to share her with you." He stubbed his cigarette out with an unhurried movement, then rose and calmly took her hand, leading her into the privacy of the bedroom.

"I called my lawyer, Philip Young, this morning. He's starting the adoption proceedings at once. Then I'll be able to help Tabby legally without uncovering private skeletons or scandal. It's the easiest way."

"I'll fight this, Noah! If it takes everything I've got, I'll fight this. You have no right, now or ever, to come into our lives and tear everything apart on a whim."

"Stop whistling in the dark, Di. You know there isn't enough money in the world to stop me from what I want when I make up my mind to it," he stated calmly. "It's the only way."

"It is not!" she stormed, her mind rushing ahead toward another solution. "All right, pay for Tabby's surgery if you want, and visit her when the need to play parent becomes overwhelming. Eventually, perhaps, you'll marry and have children of your own to lavish your money upon. You certainly don't need Tabby for that!"

"I don't think you understand what I'm proposing. I want to marry you. I want to care for you as I offered to do seven years ago. I want to take care of Tabby, grow to know her. If you want her to have brothers and sisters, fine, I don't mind obliging." His smile deepened. "In return I have a hostess, mother, daughter, and peace of mind."

"I don't want to marry! I don't want to have anything to do with you, including having your children!" she cried. "And I don't give a damn about your peace of mind!"

He took her trembling hands and pulled her unresisting form into his arms. Her eyes never left his face as she silently pleaded with him to see reason.

"You know you have no choice in the matter, so why don't you just give in gracefully?" His smile was relaxed and warm, making her tense muscles go slowly limp. He had always had this strange power over her. Whenever he came too close, her calm, sane mind was thrown into turmoil. Too much had happened in the past two days for her to recover her senses now. When his lips hesitated above hers for a second, she didn't move or try to pull away. The emotions she had kept so well hidden for seven years had suddenly surfaced once more, crumbling her carefully built façade of composure and leaving her oddly weak. His lips finally claimed hers and she was stunned by the impact as her body treacherously reacted, ignoring the feeble signals from her frozen mind. Her hands clung to his waist, raising his knit sweater so she could feel his firm warm skin beneath her palms. She was caught up in her physical response to him and strangely exhilarated by the feel of his heart beating in quickened unison with her own.

"It won't be as bad as you try to believe, Di." He nuzzled against the softness of her cheek, breathing in the scent of her skin. "We already know you respond to me, to my touch." His hands traveled from her waist to the curve of her breasts, his thumbs gently caressing her already tingling nipples. "See?" He nibbled her earlobe. "In another five minutes I could make you want me just as much as I want you." His voice was lost in the night-colored silk of her hair as he pressed his thighs to hers, letting her feel his awakened desire. She couldn't move, couldn't resist him. The warm, hungry feeling that rushed through her veins had to be satisfied and he alone held the power to release her. Only *his* hands could make her hot and cold at the same time. Only *his* body could awaken her desire for completeness. She should have known. Hadn't he proved it to her many years ago?

Nimble fingers unzipped her dress and pushed it off her slim shoulders, letting it fall with a swish to the carpeted floor. Somehow her bra was unhooked, freeing her breasts for his questing hands. She held him tight, straining herself to him with a crazy abandon. All thoughts were gone, to be replaced with one single emotion. She wanted more; she wanted him.

His moist firm mouth demanded a response she willingly gave. One hand gently caressed her breast while the other slid down her flat, taut stomach to the swell of her hips, then lowered the lacy elastic band of her black panties, finding what he had been seeking, and receiving a muffled sigh of ecstasy for his persistence in gaining the prize.

"My God, Di. You're beautiful. Who would ever have thought there was still a wonderful hot-blooded woman beneath that nunlike exterior?" His hands lightly traced a path over her skin, leaving heat wherever he touched, drawing her closer to the brink . . . of what?

"Hold me, Dianna. Hold me and touch me like I'm touching you, darling," he breathed into her ear, and mindlessly she obeyed, her hands reaching to eliminate the fabric between them.

"You've got company, Mr. Weston. Kitty Sinclair is waiting to see you in the hallway." Mrs. Frank's voice came in muffled tones from outside the door, stopping all motion. Dianna's breath was shallow and her senses were drugged. As she tried to gather her jumbled thoughts together Noah hesitated, then gave her a quick kiss on the tip of her nose.

"Game's called due to interference. Thank your fairy godmother, Dianna, because you won't be so lucky again." His husky voice made it clear he had been shaken too. Sure hands quickly buttoned his shirt and pushed the edge into the waistband of his pants before he quirked an eyebrow in her direction. She was standing in the middle of the bedroom, where he had left her. "Dianna?"

She glanced down, suddenly realizing she was naked. "I'm leaving," she muttered through her teeth, unable to look at him for fear of seeing that mocking smile. She had played right into his hands. Well, she had left him once before—the same prescription would work again.

"You're not going anywhere. I'll be right back."

"Don't tell me the great Mr. Weston is afraid I might disappear into thin air?" she taunted, not sure whether she was trying to regain her composure or make him lose his.

"Don't even try." His voice hardened ruthlessly. "This time there's nowhere you could go that I wouldn't be able to find you." He stared through her, then turned and strode from the room toward the front door.

Dianna used the small modern tan phone in Noah's room, her fingers trembling as she pushed the white buttons. She listened impatiently to the rings: two, three, four. Would June never answer?

"Hello?" June sounded carefree and happy, as though she had just shared a joke with someone.

"June?" Dianna's voice cracked, and both hands clutched the receiver tightly as she tried to calm her fears.

"Hi, Dianna. Are you feeling better now, honey? We were worried last night until Noah called and told us how sick you were. I'm so sorry. I remember how those headaches used to affect you."

Dianna broke into June's ramblings. "June, did Noah come by your house this morning?"

There was a moment's hesitation before her sister answered, her voice holding a forced brightness. "Why, yes. Didn't he tell you? I assumed he had your permission to meet Tabby."

"What happened?"

"Well, he talked to David and me first. He . . . he asked a lot of questions about you and Tabby." June halted.

"Go on!" Dianna exclaimed impatiently.

"Then he met Tabby. They talked for a while, and he took her for a drive. I don't know what he said to her, but she's positively glowing. They really hit it off, Di. I guess she needed a man in her life, just like the rest of us. Anyway, when he turned on that charm there was nothing she could do but succumb."

"Oh, my God," Dianna muttered.

"Is everything all right? Has something gone wrong?" June's voice sounded worried now. What did June have to be worried about, Dianna thought bitterly. June wasn't in a mess; she was!

"I'll talk to you later. As soon as I can." Her throat choked. She couldn't ask David to come and get her. Noah had effectively blocked that exit. The last door had closed and she was sealed in a tomb. It was a tomb as large as the world, but sealed just the same. There was no escaping: Noah had seen to that.

4

It was quiet. Not even the soft sounds of Mrs. Frank's preparations for dinner penetrated the bedroom. Dianna sat in the bentwood rocker and stared out at the rooftop garden of the penthouse apartment. The large windows allowed the late afternoon sun to warm the room with a bright cheeriness, but Dianna didn't notice. She had completed dressing and was now waiting calmly for whatever would happen next.

Her eyes were clouded with visions of the past that reached out to overwhelm her. She was tired—too tired to pit herself against the force of a will much stronger than hers. She had already suffered for trying. Her emotions had been put into deep freeze by the shock of the past two days' events and she was having trouble thinking straight.

Her mind said that she was thankful for the interruption earlier, but her body still ached for the fulfillment of Noah's lovemaking. Just as it had seven years ago, when Noah had last held her in his arms. It was frightening. At that time she had thought all men were uncaring animals. She had imagined that any contact with a man would disgust and degrade her as much as being raped had. That was where her thinking had gone wrong. She had known Noah's tender kisses after the rape. She had known his gentle hands on her skin as he washed her bruised body and dried her tears, the reassurance of his understanding words as he told her she was still a fine, wonderful person. She had known the sweetness of his lovemaking. . . .

That night—that night Noah had carried her up to the apartment from the car where Charles had been so hurting. She had hidden her face in Noah's shoulder, softly moaning as he held her in the elevator, making soothing sounds while waiting impatiently for the elevator to reach its destination at the top of the building. He had undressed her and washed her down from a basin of warm water at her bedside. The washcloth was clean and the soap sweet smelling to erase the scent of pine after-shave and wine. Her mumblings continued and the tears trickled down her face as he drew the story from her. When she had choked out the last words, he held her like a baby until she had fallen asleep in his arms, content in his impersonal, soothing touch. She awoke drowsily every few hours only to fall asleep again, afraid to face the daylight and the problems it would bring. She wanted to remain unconscious until the pain was gone. Only it would not go away. It was irreversible.

The large blue bruises disappeared within a few days, turning yellow, then fading away. But her soul was bruised, too. She had been violated in the worst possible way.

She knew that the violation had nothing to do with making love. She wasn't even sure it had anything to do with sex—at least, not as she had thought of it. Charles had lashed out at her because she was there. She knew that, yet she couldn't feel sympathy or understanding for what he had done. All she could feel was a flame of hatred burning deep in the pit of her stomach like acid on metal.

One night about a week later she had awakened to find the apartment in darkness. Her nerves tensed immediately and she knew she couldn't sleep any longer. Slowly she crept from bed and made her way to the living room. Moonlight streamed through the glass walls, illuminating the stark forms of the furniture. It must have been very late, for most of the lights of the city were darkened, leaving eerie holes in the landscape.

Suddenly panic like she had never known before welled up in her throat and she let out a scream, falling to the floor as she finally allowed the terrifying emotions that had built up over the past days to explode within her. Sobs shook her slight frame, deep sobs that racked her insides. She rubbed her skin abrasively against the rough carpet. She was so dirty, so unclean! God help her, she would never be clean again! Never!

Noah had come from out of nowhere and pulled her

into his arms. He rocked her back and forth soothingly, attempting to keep her hands from hurting herself further. His deep-timbered voice finally broke through the mist of agony surrounding her and he was able to calm her before leading her back to bed. Her hands clung to him as she sobbed out the feelings she had kept locked inside. She was finally becoming part of the world again and it hurt.

"My God, I'm so dirty, Noah! So dirty!" she had cried over and over.

"Listen to me!" he stated firmly, kneeling before her and holding her hands as she sat on the side of the bed. "You are not dirty. You are you, with the same body you had before. Look at what happened, meet it, and then you can cope with it." She shook her head as tears continued to course down her cheeks unheeded. She knew he didn't understand, but she needed him anyway. She held tight to his hands, afraid to let him go. As long as he was there the overwhelming panic would not return.

"If you had fought off a burglar and he had hit you, would you have been any different?" he persisted as she stared at him, hazel eyes shining with hurt and glistening tears. "No. You'd still be the same Dianna, except that you would have had a bad experience. You can't blame yourself for someone else's behavior. It's not fair to yourself or Charles. He deserves to hold all the blame, and if you continue to absorb it, then he is going to be let off too lightly. Don't do that to either of you." His voice was low. He talked to her as if she were a small child that needed to learn the fundamentals of life, lessons he would teach her. "You know that what Charles did he did out of anger and frustration. It had nothing to do with making love, Dianna. Nothing," he stated emphatically, trying to break through the shell she seemed to be hiding behind.

"Noah?" she had whispered sometime later when the sobbing had finally stopped. "Please don't leave me. Stay with me." And he had. Sometime in the early morning hours he had turned to her in his sleep and placed his arm over her shoulder to gently cup her breast. Where panic should have invaded, contentment took over. Slowly, tentatively, they both awoke and continued to explore each other, Noah allowing Dianna to take the initiative, going only as fast as she dictated. He treated her as if she were something special, precious, and she had flowered under his ministrations, delighted in his love. . . .

Could that be the real reason she had run away from him as soon as she was able? Because deep down she knew she was too unclean, too dirty for him to treat with such overwhelming tenderness? She had known then that he would be able to make her forget everything in his arms. Noah had the power to erase that one night of horror, but if that was so, could she respond to anyone or just to Noah? Was that the real reason behind her cloistered life? Was she afraid to find out?

Questions tumbled over one another, confusing her more, and she brushed a hand over her forehead as if to stop her own inquisition. It didn't really matter. All that mattered was getting Tabby well. Until then she would do whatever was needed in order for Tabby to survive. Dianna stood and walked to the window, where the sun played on her raven-black hair, turning it blue with highlights.

The air was suddenly charged with electricity and Dianna instinctively knew Noah had entered the room. She could feel him standing directly behind her. He was the one object her senses were acutely aware of, as though she were a compass attracted to a large magnetic force.

"Soul-searching?" His warm breath faintly ruffled her loosely flowing hair.

"Would it change your mind about marrying me?" Dianna didn't turn. She wasn't ready to face him yet.

"No. Nor would hysterics."

"Then I'll do neither."

"Good. There's enough to do right now without throwing tantrums."

"Such as?"

"Going to your house to pack a few things for the week. Later you can use my account at Neiman-Marcus to buy whatever you and Tabby need."

She turned slowly, facing him. As always, it startled her to see how tall and broad he was. He exuded a male aura that irritated her as much as it drew her to him. It made her feel small, inadequate, and constantly on the defensive.

"Has Catherine gone?"

"Would you be jealous if I said no?"

"I don't really feel one way or the other. She's your choice. I just hope you won't be too obvious about it in the future. Children need stability, and Tabby's could be undermined by your actions."

"Obvious about what?"

He was playing a cat-and-mouse game but she managed to keep her voice cool. "About keeping Catherine as your mistress after our marriage."

"I'll take that to mean you've accepted my proposal," he stated calmly, ignoring her barb.

"Yes, but I still don't understand why you're insisting on this marriage. What can you possibly hope to gain from it? Tabby is your niece—I've admitted that. But she's not your obligation and neither am I. I thought I made that clear years ago—I don't hold you responsible for what Charles did!"

"What if I'm asking you to marry me with something other than my . . . obligations in mind, Dianna? What if I'm thinking of my pleasures too?"

She gasped, blushing a deep rose as anger over-whelmed her thinking. "You would be. You're just like all the rest. I'm a fallen woman, aren't I—fair game? And the proof of my easy virtue is Tabby!"

"I think I've had more intimate proof than that," he reminded her quietly.

"Stop it!"

He raised an eyebrow in feigned surprise. "Why? Is sex supposed to be something dirty? Something to be hidden under the guise of creating children or allowing a man his animal lust, to be done but not discussed?" His laugh was tinged with huskiness. "Are you afraid to admit the pleasure you've found in my arms? You have a lot to learn about the differences between sex and love, Di, and I think it will be fun teaching you."

She couldn't speak as a strange need washed over her tired body, awakening the same desire she always felt in his presence, a need to be held and sheltered in his arms from all the fighting she had had to do to make her way in the unloving world. His eyes glittered and darkened dangerously as he read the silent plea in hers. His arms encircled her waist, but instead of lowering his mouth to claim hers, he pressed her head against the wall of his chest, cradling her like a baby. The unexpected tenderness took Dianna by surprise and unbidden tears turned to sobs as all the lost causes of yesterday were washed away by the promises of tomorrow. Noah held her gently, urging her to cry away the bitterness, and she could do nothing but obey. Everything had changed. The old way of life was gone and she could no longer cope with the new one. She was in limbo and he was her rock now just as he had been in the past.

The thought was sobering and she tried to push herself out of his arms, catching her breath on a sob. "I'm sorry," she mumbled dejectedly. "I don't know what's come over me." Her hands on his chest were stilled by his.

"Look at me, Dianna," he ordered softly, forcing her gaze up. "Do I frighten you so much?"

"Yes," she answered huskily.

"Why? Because of what happened in the past?"

"Yes." Her voice was so low he could hardly hear it, but the pain on her face could not be denied.

"We Westons have a lot to answer for," he muttered, reluctantly letting her go to run a hand through his thick dark hair, ruffling it boyishly. "Would you feel better if I said our relationship would never go any further than you wanted?"

Dianna paled. "And if I ask that it goes no further than it is now?"

He shrugged. "Then it doesn't. But I do expect you to be reasonable in your demands, Di."

"I don't understand."

"For all intents and purposes this marriage will look normal. Our relatives, Tabby, business associates, are all to believe this marriage was a love match." His flint-gray eyes locked with hers. "That may mean hand holding and kisses in public, but until you say otherwise, we'll do nothing more than that in private."

"And if I never say otherwise?" she persisted, trying to believe him yet plainly confused.

"Would you like it in writing?"

Dianna shook her head. "No. I just don't understand how a marriage of this kind could hold any appeal for you." She glanced back down at her toes. "If you really want to marry for your own pleasure, why did you choose me? Why not Catherine Sinclair?" Her questions were so artless, so childlike in contrast to her usually cool exterior that he laughed. The warmth of the sound sent shivers down her spine and she smiled at him, showing small even white teeth.

"Have you seen yourself in the mirror lately? You're beautiful. And you're a breath of fresh air. As far as physical pleasure goes—I'm willing to gamble that you'll soon want me as much as I want you." The gleam his eyes had held earlier was back and once again it brought a restriction in her breast and a deep spiraling warmth to her limbs. It wasn't an altogether unpleasant feeling and the realization disturbed her, making her withdraw once again into the cool shell of sophistication. He saw the change and released her from his embrace, leaving her strangely chilled.

"We don't have much time. I'll wait for you in the living room."

Then he was gone and the room seemed empty of life.

A feeling of lethargy filled Dianna as the midnight-blue Mercedes made its way up the freeway toward Irving.

Noah's capable hands were at the steering wheel, the music on the radio was slow and dreamy, and she closed her eyes. . . . A hand on her shoulder brought her quickly awake again and she stared into laughing gray eyes.

"We're just about there," he informed her, smiling at her sleep-bewildered expression.

"I'm sorry," she mumbled as she ran her fingers through her hair and tried to bring it to some semblance of order. She should have looked for hairpins and done it up in the usual French pleat, she thought to herself, not stopping to wonder how he'd known the way to her house.

Noah slowed down, turning into the cracked concrete drive as she stared in concentration at the small house she had called home for the past six years. She had never looked at it through someone else's eyes before and, now that she did, found it dismal. Its once white paint was flaking and yellowed. The green shutters were dull and sun bleached, some of the slats broken or missing. It was with shock that she remembered how it had looked when she'd moved in: all bright and shining, the small neglected garden crying out for a hand to tend it. Now it was as old and tired as Dianna felt.

She unlocked the door and led him into the living room, suddenly shy in Noah's company. She had been angry and tense with him before, but never shy.

She motioned to the large overstuffed chair in the corner of the small room. "If you'll have a seat, I won't be long."

"Take your time." His gaze covered the walls and furniture of the room with one all-encompassing glance before settling on her.

"I'm sorry if you're used to better surroundings, Mr. Weston, but be it ever so humble, it is my home."

"Which means?"

"Don't look down your aristocratic nose at it! If your tastes are more lavish I suggest you return to your fancy penthouse." She didn't know why she was so defensive. The furniture might have been old, but it was clean and homey and the room was pleasant to the eye.

"I was just thinking what a nice home you've made for Tabby. I know it can't have been easy. The house is more than adequate and I wasn't doing any more than satisfying my curiosity by looking around." His smile mocked her, one pitch-black brow rising. "Don't you look around when you're in someone else's home, Dianna?"

She stared at him, then turned. "I'll be through in a minute."

She walked quickly down the hall toward the bedrooms. She heard him say something about making coffee but didn't stop in her rush to get to Tabby's room. Or was she rushing to get away from him?

She grabbed a small suitcase from the back of the closet and began packing a few of Tabby's things, including her favorite books and toys, then quickly made her way to her own room and threw some items in another suitcase. It didn't take long—perhaps five minutes—but it was time enough for her to wonder how she could go through with Noah's plans. She had to talk to him, had to call this charade off!

He stood by the kitchen sink with a cup of coffee in his hand and a faraway look in his eyes, staring at the garden she and Tabby had tended so lovingly. He turned slowly at the sound of her footsteps and fixed his eyes on her, making the staccato of her footsteps falter.

"Finished?" He took another sip of hot coffee.

She cleared her throat. "I've thought a great deal about your . . . your offer, Noah. I want to call off our arrangement. I'll pay for Tabby's operation some other way—if not working for your company, then at someone else's." The silence was loud as she waited for his answer. He didn't move, just looked at her through narrowed lids. She cleared her throat again. "I'm sure you understand," she murmured, wondering how she could expect him to understand when she didn't herself.

"As far as I'm concerned there is no other company."

"What do you mean?"

"Exactly what I said. You either accept my offer or you'll never work in the computer field again." He slung a dinette chair around and sat down, resting his arms on the back as he watched her closely.

"I don't understand. Why would you want to marry me while there are so many others waiting in the wings? Why me?" she exclaimed, totally frustrated.

"It's nice to know you don't think I'm completely poisonous. I'm glad you can see that other women might not be offended at what I'm offering you," he stated dryly. "But the fact remains that I want you—and Tabby."

"Oh, of course," she retorted. "We'd both be so grateful to you for taking us out of the slums we've lived in for the past six years!"

"It certainly hasn't been a picnic, judging from the looks of things," he answered coolly, waving a hand around the small kitchen. The homey touches were visible, but it was also clear that there had been a distinct lack of money. "You've got the inside looking marvelous for what you had to work with, but the outside is in drastic need of repair. How long do you think it will be before you have to replace the roof, the shutters, repair the plumbing? I'd give you six months. It's already long overdue."

"Am I supposed to be grateful that you've offered to take me away from all this? Am I supposed to spend the rest of my life with you in order to prove just how wonderful you are and how lucky I am?"

"If that's the way you want to look at it," he replied softly as he stood and placed the chair back in its place. "Let's go."

Later that evening Dianna called Tabby and spoke to her a few minutes, explaining as clearly as possible about her upcoming marriage to Noah. Surprisingly, the little girl did not seem at all perturbed by the news. As soon as she was reassured that she would see her mother again on Tuesday, she seemed to accept the situation almost eagerly. Apparently, Dianna mused, Tabby was no more immune to Noah's charm than she was.

That night she undressed in one of Noah's guest bedrooms and took a warm, tingling shower. The water sprayed her shoulders, rinsing her clean as it washed away the aching feeling of tension. The little house in Irving held an old tub with no shower, so this was a luxury she had not been able to indulge in until now.

Her nightgown was old but clean. Slipping it over her head, she thought of all the new ones she would be able to buy whenever the whim seized her. Tabby would have the best of clothing, schools, doctors. Yes. It was all worth it. She could live pleasantly with Noah Weston for Tabby's sake. Then, when she was rested and on her feet again, they would leave and start a new life somewhere else—away from Noah's disturbing presence.

Her eyes closed and she slept with only one thought. All she had to do was keep Noah Weston at arm's length until she was ready to leave. What she wouldn't think about was why she should have to keep him there against her will. And why did it seem she was more afraid of herself than him?

Her nightmare returned with unerring accuracy, just as it had so many other times in the past.

She was in a confined space and couldn't move or get away. A faceless man frantically pressed his body against hers, pushing her soft flesh against the rich coffinlike interior. She tried desperately to fight him off, but her strength was draining quickly and panic was taking the place of reason. As she opened her mouth to scream his hand came down and stopped all breath. A bright light pierced the darkness, showering stars before her eyes just a second before her lungs produced a scream. Then—nothing, and she knew she was dead.

Dianna woke up in bed, her breathing shallow and her gown drenched with perspiration. Noah was sitting beside her, shaking her shoulders as he called out, "It's just a dream, Di. Just a bad dream!"

Dianna's eyes were dilated and glazed with too-real memories of pain and she covered her face with trembling hands. "Noah," she moaned as the nightmare slipped away, leaving her with the residue of fear, a sick, empty feeling. "Noah, hold me. Please. Hold me."

Wordlessly, he folded her into the comfort of his arms, gently rocking her like a baby. He wasn't wearing a pajama top and Dianna pressed her cold cheek against the soft curling hair on his hard chest, finding comfort in the warmth of his skin. She didn't realize she was crying until she felt the cold tears slide down her cheek. Shivers began as reaction set in and she relived the memories of the hellish nightmare. After a few minutes she finally calmed down enough to feel the closeness of their bodies and pulled away in embarrassment.

"I'm sorry I disturbed you," she said, sniffing, not looking at him.

"Don't worry. I wasn't asleep." He hesitated. "Does this happen very often?" His voice was soft and gentle, as was his hand smoothing back her tousled hair.

"Often enough." She silently wished he wouldn't touch her. It made it harder to think.

"Migraines, nightmares. What else don't I know about you?" he teased.

"You know nothing about me and less about Tabby. Perhaps it would be better if you let us go our own way." She tried to make her voice indifferent, but it cracked.

"I know you have soft skin, I know you wind your arms around me in your sleep like a kitten all cuddly and warm. I know you've been trying to raise Tabby on your own for too long and it's taken a toll on your health." His eyes had turned to smoky black as he watched her expression of fear change to desire. Noah's hand never stopped stroking the side of her face. "I know that you're not afraid of me, of my touch." His voice turned husky as his lips slowly met hers in sweet tenderness. "Oh, Dianna. Why did you ever leave me?" he murmured against the silken softness of her breast. Somehow the buttons of her nightgown had been undone and pushed aside. "I want you, Dianna. You know that. You can feel it." His eyes came level with hers, piercing her with a strange heat that filtered slowly through her body, forcing her to acknowledge his wants as hers.

She shook her head automatically. "No."

"Actions speak louder than words. If you don't want me you'll have to show me some other way. You can't look at me like that, with that light shining in your eyes, or kiss me as if you never want to stop." His voice held a deep caressing note that washed over her in waves, not allowing her time to think. The tone of his voice hypnotized, mesmerized her into powerlessness. Her hands covered his chest, then wrapped around his neck and slowly pulled his body down on hers. A voice in the back of her mind told her she was crazy, but it didn't matter. She loved the feel of his weight, the texture of his skin, the scent of his after-shave. He reached toward the lamp and with a soft click the room was dark and he was pulling her into his arms under the coolness of satin sheets.

In the slight pause of the light clicking off her mind seemed to become aware of what she was doing. She slowly came to her senses and it frightened her.

"No, don't!" she exclaimed as her mind fought for control over her body's desire.

He stiffened, hands still stroking her body. "I'm not stopping now, Dianna. You're putting up a losing battle. You want me as much as I want you, so why are you fighting?"

Her answer surprised them both. "I'm afraid," she choked. "This is wrong."

"Is it wrong to need someone and fulfill that need? No, love. What we're doing isn't wrong—not unless you make it so in your mind."

His lips teased hers, making her lose sight of the argument. "You won't have any regrets, I promise."

"Please, Noah," she begged. "It's too soon. I need more time."

Her eyes told him it was true and he gave a muffled groan before releasing her. "I made you a promise today, Dianna, and I intend to keep it. You're sure this is what you really want?"

She nodded, watching as he rose from the bed to go back into the master bedroom. "Sweet dreams," he murmured, brushing a gentle kiss across her forehead.

For one wild moment she wanted to ask him to stay, to let him bring her sweet forgetfulness. It would be heaven, she knew, but she didn't dare. It had always been this way between them. No one else could make her feel this way. No one else could make shining new memories out of old nightmares. . . .

They were at the Dallas–Ft. Worth Airport before seven on Monday morning with return reservations for late that evening.

Dianna sat quietly in the waiting area and watched Noah as he stood with his secretary, Mrs. Freeman, and gave last-minute instructions concerning the office. He glanced at her and flashed a smile while listening to his secretary's questions. The PA system announced their flight and the lines began to form. Noah raised one eyebrow in question and waited for her to join him. She gathered up her light sweater and purse, then fell in line beside him, her eyes fixed on the plane they were boarding.

"It doesn't have a rubber band for a motor, you know. It won't break down," he drawled lazily as he read the apprehension on her face.

"I didn't think it would, but I haven't flown before. It's a new experience."

"Better start getting used to new experiences, Di. You've got a lot of them in store," he teased, smiling again as he watched her lashes drop. "Besides, we always fly back and forth to the ranch for long weekends and vacations. It's easier."

"You don't drive?" she asked hesitantly, realizing how little she knew of this man who would figure so greatly in her life from now on.

"It takes too long and the roads aren't the best."

"I didn't know."

He clasped her hand, giving it a light squeeze, his gray eyes twinkling. "I know. There are so many things we each have to learn, but this is a beginning," he said softly, and her heart turned somersaults.

Noah led her on to the plane and gave her the seat next to the window. She was feeling nervous again and clung to Noah's hand, gripping it until her knuckles were white. She was so tired. The tension of the past few days was beginning to take its toll.

She had tried so hard not to show any emotion, to act calm and collected no matter what. It had been so much easier during the weekend to move and do things his way, without trying to think or reason. Besides, her mind had been a blank most of the time. Right now she was just trying to hold herself together until after Tabby's operation and recovery. By that time things would sort themselves out and she could collapse. And she didn't doubt that she was headed for some kind of breakdown. All the signs were there. Dianna had been this way once before, when she found out she was pregnant with Tabby.

"Are you all right?" Noah's voice sounded loud next to her ear as he bent over and clasped her seat belt. His hands touched her stomach and it automatically contracted, making Dianna suck in her breath in reaction. "You're so tense, Di. I don't want you to start work until Tabby's operation is out of the way and you have time to relax a little. You've got too much to cope with right now, sweetheart."

She nodded mutely, then closed her eyes and tried to relax. Perhaps if she feigned sleep he wouldn't expect conversation. She could think of nothing to say to his obvious kindness.

The wedding was simple and over quickly. It took place in one of the small white chapels off the Las Vegas strip. Noah's lips brushed her cheek in a wedding kiss, then they were off to the airport and on their way back to Dallas.

Her only emotion was relief. Relief that she would never have to worry about mounting bills again, or the roof leaking on stormy nights, or Tabby's surgery. Noah would take care of everything.

Noah smiled at her in the darkness of the plane as they sipped their wine. Neither had been hungry, neither was tired, but both seemed anxious to return home, to the apartment. Home. For so long it had meant the small white house with chipped green shutters. But no more. Now she and Tabby were beginning a new life. For better or for worse.

She stared out at the evening sky, watching the plane glide through barely visible clouds. She was content, as though she had been working all her life toward one goal and had finally attained it. Now she could reap the rewards. Then she knew. She had suspected all along, but somehow she had always managed to push the thought to the back of her mind without examining it.

She had always known that someday Noah Weston would come to her rescue. Someday, if she was good and nice and polite, she would be rewarded by Noah stepping through the door and announcing that he would take over the helm of her small, slightly weather-beaten raft of life. Oh, she would put up the expected resistance, but he would overrule. And she would allow him to.

She realized now that that was why she had applied to Wescomp for a job—not for the money, not for the opportunity to advance her career, not even for the medical insurance to cover Tabby's operation. She had done it to be close to Noah again, to correct the mistake she'd made seven years ago when she'd run away from him.

What made it so funny was that she knew that he knew. He had known for a long time that this same thing would happen and all they were doing was playing it through to the end, like two actors who knew their parts so well they lived them. Almost. But what was Noah's motivation? Why did he do the things he did? Out of love? Somehow she doubted it. Why then? Tabby? She didn't want to know the answer yet. Later, much later, she would think about it.

The Wescomp limousine was at the curb as they walked through the glass doors of the airport lobby. Jimmy, the chauffeur, was waiting for them with a smile as big as a quarter moon.

"Congratulations, Mr. and Mrs. Weston," he welcomed them, opening the rear door with a flourish. His tone was respectful, but there was a certain amount of relaxed banter in his manner too, and it made Dianna feel more at home as she stepped into the back seat, making room for Noah to join her.

"Everything go all right today, Jimmy?"

The chauffeur gave Noah an intense look before turning to start the car. "The canary seemed to like her new bauble, all right. The price seemed to fit right into what she thought she was worth. Expensive."

"Good."

Noah's brow cleared and Dianna wondered at the exchange but was too tired and content to delve into it now. Let Noah do the worrying, if there was any. After all, that's what he wanted to do. She leaned back, resting her head on the soft velour upholstery. It was good to feel the smooth hum of the car as it sped down the highway toward their apartment. Toward home.

In the past four days she had gone to a party, met Noah, and married. No wonder she was tired! But it was a good feeling, as though she had just won a race. It had been a matter of endurance, but the victory was sweet.

"Too tired, Mrs. Weston?" Noah's lips brushed her palm.

"Too tired for what, Mr. Weston?" she asked innocently.

"Too tired for anything I may have in mind," he teased, grinning as he watched the streetlights show up her reddened cheeks.

They entered through the lobby of Wescomp, Noah leading the way to the elevator that took them up to the apartment. It was quiet, but there was an excitement in the air that seemed to intensify the electricity between them.

He led her through the apartment door, down the hall, and directly into the master bedroom, holding her by the shoulders as he turned her to face him. His voice was low and firm. "We're married now, Dianna, and there's no going back."

She nodded slowly as his words washed over her. He was making her admit to herself just how aware of him she was, and it was frightening.

"There will be no *holding* back either. If we're to make a lasting marriage we both have to try. Understand?"

Again she nodded.

"No more secrets, no more skeletons in the closet. I'll take care of you and Tabby the best I can, but that's my price." His smoky eyes locked with hers, telling her something that remained unsaid—but what?

"I have no secrets," she stated simply.

"Yes, you do. And so do I. But from now on we'll explore them together. I don't want a synopsis of your past sins any more than you want one of mine. But in the future, as questions arise, I expect honesty and trust."

He began unbuttoning her shirtwaist, his burning eyes holding her still, his hands never fumbling with the small covered buttons. Her belt was unfastened and the pale gray dress slid to the floor. Dianna started to retreat, but his hands held her as they clasped her waist. "No, Dianna. Stay where you are," he ordered softly.

He unsnapped her bra and it too fell to the plush carpeting. Dianna didn't move—only her panties protected her from his raking gaze.

"Beautiful," he murmured, and for some reason she was no longer embarrassed, only proud. He slipped the panties down and she stepped out of them gracefully, hesitating before moving to unbutton his shirt, caressing his skin lightly with her fingertips, then reaching for his belt buckle, undressing him as he had undressed her.

There was no rush, no hurry. They had all the time in the world. They smiled unspoken words to each other and the tension mounted, drawing them together. Soon they were both naked in the bright room and neither showed the slightest tremor of embarrassment as they gazed at each other.

He drew her slowly into his arms so flesh could brush flesh. "Frightened?" he asked softly as he held her close, letting her feel his need for her.

"No," she whispered, a tremor in her voice.

"Not even a little?" His breath teased her ear as his hands roamed her back and hips, molding her closely to the contours of his lean body, allowing her to become familiar with the intimate differences between male and female.

"A little," she admitted.

His lips bent to tease a taut dusky pink nipple, hands searching other pleasure points. She gasped at the feeling of warm molten lead overwhelming her and held tight to his shoulders as his tongue made a path down her ribs to her flat stomach.

"No! Noah!" she cried, suddenly frightened. He raised shining black eyes to her, reluctantly straightening with a sigh. A small rueful smile played over his mouth.

"I keep forgetting. I'll bide my time, Dianna. We have all the time in the world now." And he kissed her, slowly, with drugging passion, his hands sliding over her soft skin at will to send small flames of desire through her body. It was wonderful, this feeling of belonging that winged through her veins and made her blood hot and cold at the same time. Muscles contracted and expanded with the wonder of his knowing touch; her head was dizzy with his kisses. Her own hands weren't idle, moving over his body with the instinctive sense of the blind. She closed her eyes to the brightness of the light, to him—only feeling, touching.

"Open your eyes, Dianna."

She shook her head.

"Open them. I want to see you," he ordered softly, and she finally obeyed.

"Do you love me? Is that why you agreed to marry me?"

Her eyes were blank—the question had not registered.

"Answer me, Dianna. Do you love me?"

"Yes." She closed her eyes and pulled his mouth toward hers, catching only a glimpse of his victorious smile.

"Then let me love you." He picked her up and carried her to the bed, laying her gently on it before turning out the light.

The phone on the nightstand jangled and Dianna reached for it without a second thought, trying to hush it quickly so the spell they had woven would not be broken.

"Hello."

There was a moment of silence before a voice laced with tears answered vindictively, "Well, well, well. Mrs. Goody Two-Shoes is in residence already. Put your husband on the line, sweetie—his well-paid mistress needs a word with him."

5

The spell had been broken, bringing reality back with a crashing bang. Dianna held the receiver toward Noah, who sat beside her, puzzlement written on his face.

"It's Catherine Sinclair. She wants to talk to you," Dianna said in a cold, dead voice, retreating into a shell made long ago. Withdraw and retreat—that was her only possible course of action. She should have known better. . . .

Noah sat on the edge of the bed and switched on the small reading lamp, his eyes noting the change in Dianna, knowing in advance what had brought it about. He had hoped Jimmy's errand would eliminate this particular problem. His face took on a shuttered look as he accepted the receiver from her outstretched hand. Dianna fell back on the pillows to cover her eyes with trembling fingers while he answered.

"Noah Weston here."

Catherine seemed to do most of the talking, eliciting only terse monosyllables from the angry man on the bed. "When?" A pause. "Where?" Another pause. "Dammit, Kitty! I—all right. I'll be right there. Yes, yes. I'll have Philip meet us there," he said resignedly. "Meanwhile, don't panic, and keep your mouth shut."

Dianna heard the click as the receiver was placed back on its cradle. "Di." He hadn't yet moved to get dressed as she had expected.

"Go on, Noah. Your well-paid mistress needs you far more than I do." Her voice was level, laced with contempt.

He didn't know the scorn was directed at herself, not him. He sighed heavily. "Listen, Dianna."

"Listen to what? An excuse for going to your mistress on our wedding night? Or should I listen to promises about making this farce of a marriage work?" Her voice rose, becoming louder with every word.

She wanted to lash out at him, hurt him as Catherine's words had stabbed her. Her laugh was short and sharp. "At least this way you won't need servicing like some prize stud, and I won't feel obligated by duty to fulfill your needs. You'll still have Catherine. God knows she's probably experienced enough to perform whatever kind of sex you have a craving for!"

"So," he said softly, "the tiger replaces the purring kitten again. I wondered how long the docile-wife routine would last."

"I was just trying to make the best of a bad situation for Tabby's sake."

"Then, for Tabby's sake, you had better continue," he said harshly as he stood and grabbed his clothing. He wasn't the least embarrassed by his nudity as he dressed in front of her. She couldn't help noticing how flat his stomach was, how firm the muscles of his thighs, how well built . . .

He turned and for a split second held her eyes with his. "She's in jail, Dianna. Jail! She was at a party that was busted by the police." He buttoned his shirt with quick fingers and ran a hand through already mussed hair. Somehow he looked younger, more vulnerable.

"Jail?" Dianna repeated stupidly.

"Yes, dammit! Jail!"

"Why was the party busted?"

His belt was buckled and he reached for his socks. "Drugs, illegal gambling—you name it," he answered exasperatedly as he reached for the telephone and jabbed at the numbers on the dial. "She's just a mixed-up kid. I've got to do whatever I can to . . . Hello, Philip?" His voice changed completely to that of a man in charge. Gone was the husband, the lover. Was it all an act? Was this the real Noah Weston?

She listened to the conversation as he explained the situation to his lawyer in a few clear, well-chosen words.

"Yes, the whole thing is a mess. We'll bring Kitty back here before worrying about anything else."

"No!" Dianna exclaimed, but he ignored her.

Noah hung up the phone and stared at her, his face hard and uncompromising. "If I can get her out on bail, Catherine is coming here for the night, or what's left of it. You won't have to see her, if that's what's worrying you."

He stood. "I expect you to tolerate the situation, just as I will."

"You do what you want! Just don't expect me to be here to welcome you both."

"You'll be here. The guard at the door will have orders not to allow you to leave. Make the best of it, Di. I don't like the situation any better than you, but there's no choice in the matter right now."

Dianna continued as if she had never heard him, one part of her not believing she was saying such ugly things, while another part of her was too hurt to stop. "When you said you could offer us everything, I didn't know just what that encompassed, did I?" She sat up and her unpinned hair tumbled in wild disorder about her slim shoulders, making her look like a temptress and a vulnerable child at the same time. "You have all sorts of things you can teach Tabby, don't you? Sex, mistresses, drugs, excesses of money, rape—the list is endless!"

"You don't know what you're saying." His voice was barely controlled.

"You're right, I don't! But if I'm here long enough I'm sure I'll find out."

"You'd make a perfect witch." Noah turned and opened the bedroom door. "I'll be back later. I don't have to tell you not to wait up for me. I can see wifely concern written all over your face." He halted. "Don't try to leave."

"I don't have much choice, do I?"

"No, you have no choice. Not if you want what's best for Tabby."

"You're ruthless, aren't you, Noah? What if other people's plans don't coincide with yours? Are they always relegated to second place?"

"You're doing so well analyzing my character, why should I bother to clutter your mind with facts?"

He was gone and Dianna sat in the darkened room alone. Her body still craved his hands, his touch, but her mind fought over and over against her need for him. He was a heartless bully or a saint, and Dianna's tired mind couldn't distinguish which.

When she awakened the next morning Catherine Sinclair was not in the apartment. Neither was Noah. Presumably he would be at work by now, she told herself.

Mrs. Frank had grapefruit, bacon, eggs, and pancakes waiting for her as she walked into the kitchen, and no amount of explaining about light breakfasts could convince the older woman that this was one meal Dianna could do without.

She finally sat down and, with one eye on the clock, tried to do justice to Mrs. Frank's cooking. June and David were bringing Tabby sometime early this afternoon and Dianna pushed everything but this single thought out of her mind. Tabby was all that mattered. It wasn't important where Noah had spent the night or where he was at this moment.

She put down her fork and sighed. There was no way she could eat right now—her stomach was churning too much. She almost wished she could start work, where at least she would be kept too busy to think much. Dianna reached for her cigarettes and walked into the living room, her mind back on the train of thought that had begun last night.

Without really wanting to, she relived those moments in Noah's arms and her face burned as she remembered how she had told him she loved him, only to have him say he wanted to make love to her. It wasn't the same at all. She stared at an ad in the magazine she was leafing through, making no sense of the blurred type. She needed something sane and sensible to hang on to in her Alice in Wonderland world. Soon Tabby would be there. . . .

Once June, David, and Tabby arrived, the afternoon passed quickly. June was awed by the penthouse apartment and even David took a little time to become accustomed to sitting back in richly upholstered furniture and staring at original artwork on the walls. Tabby, however, took everything in stride, as children do.

"Just imagine! I've passed this building often, but I never knew anything like this existed on the top!" June twisted sideways on the couch to stare out the large expanse of glass to the patio, where redwood planters stood filled with shrubs and shiny-leafed foliage, and white enameled lounge furniture invited one to sit and relax. At the edge of the balcony was a large waterfall that tinkled with soft rushing water over moss-covered stones. It was artificial but looked as if it had been placed there by nature.

"Yes, it is beautiful, isn't it?" Most of Dianna's attention was on Tabby and her reaction to the surroundings, but the small girl seemed almost oblivious to the unaccustomed luxury around her. It puzzled Dianna. Her daughter seemed to be waiting for something, or someone.

"I always said you should have contacted Noah Weston before now, and I was right! What a Cinderella story. I just don't understand why you didn't do this seven years ago!" June's sly glance irritated Dianna, but she brushed the feeling aside as she realized just how hard her independence had been on June and David. They had helped her buy her little house, acted as a buffer between Dianna and her parents before Tabby's birth, even baby-sat in a pinch. The extra responsibility must have been a strain, but surprisingly, Dianna had never been conscious of that fact before. "And you have to admit, Dianna, Noah is one good-looking man. If it weren't for the fact that I'm madly in love with my own husband . . ." She smiled at David, who made a face at her.

"You'd better say that," he growled in mock severity.

Tabby sat next to her mother on the couch, glancing through a magazine with the expression of a patient adult. "Did you water my plants, Mommy?"

"Yes, darling." She took a deep breath of air, her voice becoming more resolute. "Tabby, you know that Noah and I are married now, right?" She gave her a hug. "I want to talk to you about how things will be, now that we'll all be living together."

"Have you seen the ranch and picked out a place for my new garden?" Tabby's face flushed with excitement. "Noah says it can be as big as I want it."

"Noah says?"

"We, well, I . . ." June stammered as she glanced at David for support.

"Hi, Monkey." Noah lounged in the doorway, his brown suit jacket slung over his shoulder and hooked by lean fingers. His tan-colored shirt and gold striped tie were loosened to expose the muscled column of his throat. He looked tired, but his eyes held an amused glint that bordered on mockery.

"Hi, Noah." Tabby grinned. "Mom doesn't know about my garden at the ranch."

Noah draped his coat over the back of a chair and stepped into the room. "Not yet, sweetheart. I haven't had a chance to tell her." He glanced at Dianna. "It's been a little busy around here, so you'll have to fill her in for me, okay?"

He turned and shook hands with David and greeted June with a warm smile. Dianna listened to Tabby discuss her weekend with her cousins, which had been a rare treat, but her eyes followed Noah to the bar, where he was mixing drinks while carrying on a casual conversation with David. She didn't notice June's frown. She wasn't aware of anything but Noah. He stood, drink in hand, and chatted as if with an old friend, occasionally glancing down to give Tabby a wink.

"Can I tell Mommy our secret now?" Tabby walked up to Noah, stopping at the toes of his shoes and tilting her head back to look up. Her eyes were twinkling as she gave his hand a squeeze and his smile warmed at her childish expression of exuberance.

"I think the time is right, don't you? This way if your mother is mad at me she won't be able to hit me in front of your aunt and uncle." He bent down and said in a stage whisper, "She won't want to make a scene."

Tabby placed her hand on his taut stomach and pushed playfully, batting her lashes and flirting with the innocence of a child. "Oh, you!" she laughed. "Mommy couldn't be mad at you—you're too nice." She smiled disarmingly at her mother. "Isn't he, Mommy?"

Dianna couldn't answer. The thoughts that tumbled over each other in her head would not come out in words. All she could do was nod her head.

"Aren't you going to tell your mom the secret, Tabby?" June asked brightly, stepping into the breach of silence.

"Well," Tabby began. "Noah is my daddy now and he fixed it so I'm having my surgery on Friday and I'm not to be scared 'cause afterwards I'm gonna visit his ranch, and have a garden as big as I want, and even a pony!" she exclaimed, lost in the rapture of her new life. "I'll be able to do all sorts of things I couldn't do before 'cause I needed my heart fixed." She looked up at Noah. "Right?"

"Right, sweetheart."

"You discussed all this with Tabby?" Dianna's temper suddenly came alive. "You had no right! Tabby is mine and I'll have no interference in raising her!"

Noah's voice was slow and drawling, but his eyes flashed a message she could not dismiss. "What *matters* is that Tabby's looking forward to getting better."

June twisted her hands in her lap, silently watching the struggle between two of the most stubborn people she had ever met. This was not going as planned.

"And you, June. You knew all about this when I called and you never said a word?"

Tabby interrupted calmly. "That's 'cause it was a secret until you were feeling better." She glanced up at Noah. "And Noah says I have an aunt that's gonna love me and treat me like she's my grandma—and I might have brothers and sisters, too!"

Stunned, Dianna glanced from Tabby to Noah, her mind unable to function at its normal pace. She was caught in a web of words and she couldn't seem to grasp their meaning.

Noah raised his hand against the barrage he was obviously expecting, a twinkle in his eyes as she saw the surprised and confused looks that passed around the room. "I never said a word to Tabby about brothers and sisters. That is all her own idea."

David decided this was the time to add a little levity. "We'll leave the deed to you. No sense everybody getting into the act."

Dianna slumped back into the soft cushions as they all laughed. The whole world was mad and these people were more insane than most. Didn't they realize that she had been coerced into this marriage, that all she wanted was a way out?

"But I will have brothers and sisters, won't I?" Tabby asked earnestly.

"If it makes you happy, then you'll have brothers and sisters," Noah stated calmly, ignoring Dianna's reddened face.

June gave an embarrassed laugh. "I always said Dianna should have a dozen or more. She's so good with children."

"At least they would keep her occupied. My sister used to say, 'Busy hands are happy hands.'"

"If only Mom and Dad were here. They'd be so happy to see you married . . ." June halted at the thought she should never have put into words.

"Yes, married at last," Dianna retorted bitterly. "Though I don't know if it would make all that much difference to them. They promised to throw me out if I ever came near them with my 'illegitimate child.' I believe those were Mom's words. They were a little old-fashioned, but the meaning came across loud and clear." She walked over to the large picture window, not wanting Noah to see the pain and bitterness she always felt when she remembered her parents' anger on learning of her pregnancy.

"I know they were cruel, Dianna," her sister soothed, coming up behind her, "but they came from the old school that says wrong is wrong, no matter what the circumstances."

"Yes, wrong is wrong. What happened to me was wrong, but did they bother to understand? When I needed their support, did they help?" She turned angrily to stare past June to Noah, fixing him with her accusing gaze. "No, there was no one I could trust. I had to make it on my own."

June's face was white with tension, but Noah returned Dianna's look with calm assurance. "No, Dianna, you *chose* to make it on your own." Dianna faltered, understanding the words that had meaning only for her.

"Could I see Tabby's room before we leave?" June asked, hoping to change the awkward subject that she had unwittingly brought up. Dianna was instantly contrite, already regretting her show of temper in front of Tabby and Noah. She smiled sadly at her sister.

"Of course." Dianna led the way across the living room, down the hall, and into the bedroom reserved for Tabby. "There are four bedrooms in all. Tabby's room is next to mine."

June stuck her head around the door before entering the large bedroom. It was decorated in amethyst and green, which coordinated with the violet and leaf design on one wallpapered wall. The bed was canopied and the coverlet was of white eyelet, as were the curtains. The carpet was a pale amethyst and the pictures that hung on the wall picked up the same hue. But the furniture added the prettiest touch of all. It was French Provincial in design, but done in a pale antique green.

"Oh, how beautiful!" June declared as she stared in awe at her surroundings. "It's just like a little girl's room should be!" June trailed a finger over a small vase of fresh daisies sitting on the nightstand. Flowers for a little girl of six. Somehow it seemed too thoughtful for an uncle to provide so much for his niece.

"What really happened when Noah went to your house on Saturday?" Dianna asked quietly.

"What a silly question!"

"Answer me."

June turned quickly, tilting her chin determinedly at her sister. "I've already told you. He asked who Tabby's father was, and I told him. Then he took Tabby out for a ride and when he came back he told us that he planned to marry you." June's voice wavered, pleading with her to understand.

"You told him that Charles was Tabby's father?"

"Yes, but he didn't want to believe it at first—he kept insisting there must have been someone else, someone after the rape. Up till then David had been doing most of the talking, but I couldn't let him say those things about you. He was trying to make it seem as though you were some kind of loose woman, when all those years it was his family that was responsible for the suffering you went through. I told him just what I thought of him then." At her sister's stunned look, June hesitated before continuing. "I told him Tabby was his responsibility and that if he was any kind of a man he'd support you both!"

"Oh, my God," Dianna whispered. "June, tell me the truth. How did Noah know to call you that night when I was sick?"

June blanched at the question, answering her sister in a low monotone. "I'd spoken to him before about you, Di. About a week ago. It seems he hired a private detective to find out all about you when you reapplied to Wescomp. The detective gave him my number and when he called he sounded so distraught I didn't have the heart to hang up. He said he'd lost you once before and he didn't intend to make the same mistake twice. I—I answered all his questions. I thought he deserved to know the truth."

"He knew." Dianna shook her head slowly from side to side. The night of the cocktail party, when he had brought her up here, he had already known the answers to his questions. He had played with her like a cat with a very tired mouse.

"I couldn't tell you, Dianna. You do see that, don't you? I wanted to, just before the cocktail party, but you got so angry at the idea of Noah finding out about Tabby. I didn't dare! Someone had to do something. He should have been with you all along, not just now! It was his brother that was responsible for Tabby—it's only right that he should care for you both!"

Hysteria bubbled in her throat. All this time when she had been feeling trapped by this farce of a marriage, it was really Noah who had been snared! He was the one who had been forced to take responsibility for his dead brother's child! He was the one who had had June forcibly reminding him of his obligations.

She chuckled, her chuckle turning into laughter as unheeded tears streamed down her cheeks and throat to dampen the neckline of her dress. She laughed softly, but she couldn't stop. Grabbing the side of the bed and sitting down, she held her aching stomach as the laughter shook her. "Don't you see?" Dianna gurgled as her sister stared in amazement. "It's all so funny! All this time I thought he trapped me, but it was really the other way around! I forced him to pay his brother's account, be his brother's keeper. Tabby, you, me—we all forced him into a marriage he didn't want!"

The laughter died in her throat and the tears turned to sobs. Dianna cradled her head in trembling hands as tears poured through her fingers.

"I did it for you," June whispered. "I thought it would help. It did, didn't it? Tabby's going to have her surgery, you're taken care of, you have a beautiful home . . ." She broke off as Dianna looked up, incredulous.

"You mean that as long as I'm taken care of it doesn't matter whether I love him or he loves me?" She watched June's mouth snap shut. "It's all right that on our wedding night he left me to go to his mistress? Would you be half as happy if David didn't love you? If he had other women?"

"No!"

"Yes!" Dianna mimicked. "We were raised wrong, June. We were raised to expect things that just aren't real. 'Be good and good things will come to you. Turn the other cheek.' There must be a million little sayings Mother used, and they're all false! The only thing that makes this whole mess meaningful is Tabby. I don't care about anyone else—not even you!"

Dianna stood and walked to the bathroom, closing the door, and her mind, to June's imploring words. She just couldn't take any more!

6

It could have been anywhere between five minutes to an hour since Dianna had slammed the door on June. She didn't know. She sat on the edge of the bathtub and stared into the tiled shower stall until her limbs cried out for release from their stiff position. She finally stood and stared into the mirror, seeing the puffiness tears had made. When the door opened, she continued to blot her eyes with cool water, ignoring Noah's presence.

"June told me what happened."

She folded the dampened towel and placed it carefully on the rack before turning to face him. His brows were drawn together in a dark frown to frame questioning gray-black eyes. "She never could keep a secret—even as a child."

"No one can *make* me do anything, Dianna."

She ignored the implication. "That was proved best last night. You wouldn't have gone to Catherine if you didn't want to."

"If I didn't know better, I'd say you were jealous."

She replaced a loose pin in her French pleat. "You do know better, though."

"And what about you? Do you ever operate under a sense of duty or responsibility for anyone besides Tabby?"

"What I feel for Tabby is probably foreign to you. It's called love." Dianna remained calm. It was like a chess game—which piece would he move next?

"Are you saying self-sacrifice is automatic proof of love?" He quirked an eyebrow as he casually leaned against the counter and crossed his arms, perfectly relaxed.

"Have you been reading up on the subject? You wouldn't try to tell me you have firsthand knowledge of it, would you? Is that what you mistakenly call the arrangement you have with Catherine?" She smiled as she matched his casual attitude, leaning against the shower door. "It must have been misspelled in my book. We used to call it 'lust'." White queen takes black bishop.

He shrugged. "Lust is as good a word as any other for our relationship. She needed help with her career and I needed an occasional bed partner. We both knew the rules and based our relationship on those needs."

"Then perhaps you'd better explain the rules to Catherine. I have the distinct feeling she had other plans for you. That is, if you're really being honest."

Noah ran a hand through his black hair, ruffling its usual neatness. "I never passed myself off as a monk. I just happen to prefer a set arrangement to hunting for a stranger every time I feel the urge."

"Is that why you married me?" She gave him a look of pure innocence. "I remember only too well the days when you weren't so lazy. You would pull someone off the street, clean her up, take her to bed, then set her up in a small retirement home for cast-off lovers." Check.

"What exactly do you mean by that?"

"I don't want to discuss it." She pushed away from the shower door, her eyes sparkling with diamond-hard hate. "I never want to be reminded of that time again."

"No. You only want to hold on to what Charles did to you, like a talisman. As long as you remember that, you'll never let yourself get out of control, never have to give of yourself to another man. A perfect excuse. It certainly makes life easier, if monotonous."

"Get out!" she gritted between clenched teeth.

"Why should I leave? You're my wife now, remember?" His voice held a hint of amusement.

"Haven't you hurt me enough yet?" she choked. Checkmate.

The smile was wiped from his face as he backed away to place his hand on the doorknob.

"Dinner will be ready in fifteen minutes." He left.

Why didn't she feel victorious? She had won, hadn't she?

Dianna reluctantly entered the living room to find June and David gone, and Tabby engrossed in conversation with Noah. Tabby was much too busy with him to notice Dianna's silence. The two of them had been seriously discussing Tabby's garden and had progressed to the point of deciding where to put which plants. Noah had drawn a sketch of the grounds, pointing out the best places to dig the beds of flowers and vegetables that Tabby wanted to try her hand at. They were becoming closer every minute and Dianna felt like an outsider.

Later, after dinner, Dianna mechanically readied Tabby for bed. Before slipping between the covers, Tabby insisted on saying good night to Noah. He promptly put the newspaper he had been reading down when he saw her enter the room, his face a broad smile as she walked toward him in her blue-checked gingham nightgown. Her face scrubbed, her hair neatly braided, she looked like the perfect picture of a little girl. Dianna watched from the doorway, not wanting to be drawn into the intimate family setting they made, but oddly jealous of their close companionship.

"Are you going to read the paper when Mommy finishes tucking me in bed?" Tabby asked.

"I don't know, sweetheart. Why?"

"Well, 'cause mommies and daddies are supposed to sit on the couch and talk about the children after the children go to bed. Then the daddies watch television while the mommies sew," she explained patiently.

"Where do you get your information?" Noah teased, lightly pulling a long corn-colored pigtail.

"From the kids at school," she answered artlessly. "An' usually when I go to bed Mommy sews or reads the bills, but she won't have to read the bills anymore 'cause now we have you. Right?"

"Right. Now go to bed so Mommy and I can talk about you." Noah lifted the small child into his arms and carried her into her new bedroom, placing her gently between the sheets. Bending down, he gave her a light kiss on the forehead. "Good night, Tabby. If you need anything, you know where we are."

"Okay . . . Daddy." She giggled impishly and Dianna's heart contracted with love.

After she tucked the little girl in bed and sang a lullaby that had become an "always" with Tabby, Dianna retraced her steps into the living room. It was empty. Noah must have gone into the study to complete the rest of the paperwork he had talked of earlier.

She paced the carpeting to work off the excess energy that moved through her veins like a swiftly flowing stream. She was a nervous wreck, but she couldn't seem to avoid the panicky feeling that gripped her every time she and Noah were together.

Why was she behaving so strangely? What demon took possession of her, telling her things to say that she had never said before, things to do that she had never done before? Actions that had been totally foreign to her nature four days ago were now the rule rather than the exception. Everything was different except her behavior with Tabby; and that remained the same only because she spent all her energy trying to maintain the facade of stability. She would not allow Noah into her life with Tabby! She would not! She had been stupid to let them become this close, but he would get no closer if she had anything to do with it!

She stopped and looked at the image projected on the glass doors leading to the patio. The dark night made the glass into a mirror, and the reflection frightened her.

"I'm twenty-eight going on one hundred," she murmured, noticing the gauntness of her face. In years to come there would be wrinkles and sagging skin and lines of dissatisfaction etched where now there was smoothness. It won't be long—then I'll be old and miserable—and Tabby will have grown and gone. I'll be alone.

She quickly swiveled, turning her back on that image. She didn't want to think of the alternative—living with Noah and abiding by his rules. No! It was her life and she would live it as she wished!

The doorbell rang, startling her out of her reverie. She made no move to answer it. It had to be for Noah, anyway. She heard him greet someone before they both entered the living room. Their guest was a tall man—almost as tall as Noah—but his hair was the tawny gold of a lion's mane. His eyes were pale brown and they glowed in admiration as he walked toward Dianna with a hand outstretched. Noah stood to the side, wearing a small smile as he made the introductions.

"Dianna, I'd like you to meet an old friend of mine who also happens to be my attorney, Philip Young. Philip—my bride, Dianna." Dianna glanced quickly at Noah, expecting to see the mockery in his eyes, surprised when there was none.

"It's a pleasure to meet you, Mrs. Weston. The rumors of your beauty weren't exaggerated." His handclasp was firm and cool, lingering a brief second more than necessary.

"Ever since the cocktail party there've been rumors. When the newspapers get the news tomorrow there will be speculation aplenty. I wasn't able to make it to the party Friday, but since then I've had at least a half-dozen men ask me who you were."

"Enough," Noah growled as he handed his friend the attaché case he had placed on the floor. "Let's get to work, Philip."

"Right." Philip grinned at Dianna conspiratorially, making all the wrong assumptions about Noah's obvious hurry.

Dianna took out her annoyance a moment later on the cupboards as she clattered through the pantry in search of cups and saucers. Noah had sent her into the kitchen to play the hostess-bride instead of allowing her to listen to the business they were discussing. She could tell by Noah's gray-black eyes that he would brook no argument, so she had meekly left the room.

The gleaming coffeepot stopped perking and she loaded it on the tray along with the china. Carefully balancing it, she pushed at the swinging door, only to stop and hold her breath as the conversation filtered through the rooms.

"I've heard of giving a girl diamonds when you're tired of her, but interest in a record company?" Philip questioned incredulously.

"I already sent Jimmy around with a diamond bracelet yesterday as a farewell gesture. But after this blow-up I think she needs something to help her over the hump."

"Are you sure about this? Your plan has its merits, but—"

"I'm sure. She knows the business inside and out and has a good head on her shoulders when she uses it. Besides, I need someone I can trust in that spot. She'll make it pay. The one thing I can count on is Kitty's love of money."

Dianna heard Philip's answering laugh.

"How much longer before this legal problem is cleared up?" Noah questioned.

"We should be able to get her trial scheduled in the next couple weeks. What makes it prickly is that Senator Greer is caught up in this thing. If the press got their hands on any information regarding the activities at that party, they'd have a field day! But what about Catherine? Is she going to cause any trouble?" Dianna could sense a certain bitterness in his tone now.

"Catherine can be handled. I just want her out of my personal life. As a business partner she'll be perfect. As soon as this mess is cleared up, buy her a one-way ticket to Nashville." He hesitated. "Never mind, I'll explain it myself. I owe her that much." Dianna heard the clink of glasses, then Noah continued. "You and Jessie will have to come over for dinner soon. I'd like Dianna to meet her. And I want you to see Tabby, too."

"Family man at last, eh, Noah?" Philip laughed. "Never thought I'd see the day! Is that the reason you're selling . . ."

"Yes, yes," Noah interrupted impatiently. "And I don't need a lecture on that score, Philip."

"Is everyone ready for coffee?" Dianna asked cheerfully as she walked into the living room, her face placid and her wide hazel eyes dancing with green highlights. She should have been angry with Noah's arrangements for disposing of Catherine, but all she could feel was a buoyancy that he had cared enough to get rid of her. It didn't make sense, but she didn't want to examine her feelings too closely: there would be time enough for that later.

"Seems like you've found the formula for keeping

your lady in line, Noah. Care to share it?" Philip teased as he watched Dianna pour the coffee.

"It's simple. Occasionally tan their backsides."

"Hmmm. I've always found other uses for that specific part of the female anatomy!" Philip and Noah laughed as they watched Dianna blush becomingly.

Philip stayed another half hour before making his departure. When he finally rose, Dianna was sorry to see him leave. He had been their first real guest, and it was enjoyable to spend such a relaxed evening together. She began cleaning up the cups and saucers as Noah walked Philip to the door. She was drying the last of the dishes when Noah sauntered in to sit on one of the wicker kitchen stools and watch her work.

"You could have left that for Mrs. Frank."

"I can clean a dish or two without soiling my newfound reputation as a rich lady of leisure," she laughed.

She rinsed out the sink, working vigorously as she felt him come up behind her. Did his lips brush her hair? She wasn't sure, but her tensed nerves told her he was too close for comfort. Turning her head, she looked into his dark gray eyes. "Did you want something?" Her voice sounded breathless to her own ears.

His eyes gave an unspoken answer before his hands went around her waist and he drew her back against him. "Do I still scare you?"

"You're a formidable opponent."

"So are you. You throw such powerful darts, but when I want to retaliate all I see is your vulnerability." His hands tightened their hold as he turned her around in his arms and looked down at her with a softness in his eyes. "If that's not frustrating, I don't know what is." His eyes crinkled in a sad smile. "Poor Dianna. Is it so hard to give our marriage a try without looking for problems under every tree and rock?"

"Is that what you think I'm doing?"

"Aren't you?" His hand cupped the nape of her slender neck, stroking her smooth skin softly and at the same time urging her head to tilt up to his.

"I don't know."

"Why don't we start from the beginning again, Dianna? If we both try to understand one another then perhaps we won't always be jumping to the wrong conclusions." His thumb rubbed against the tender skin just under her earlobe. "For Tabby's sake?"

"Tabby?" Her thoughts were incoherent. His hands and low, husky voice were working a languorous spell on her. He was too close—much too close.

"She wants to be part of a family as much as I do. If we have you in our corner we just might get our wish." His voice grew even more husky. "Give us a try?"

Dianna slowly nodded her head, looking at the dark hair curling just below his throat. He tilted her chin higher and captured her eyes with his, sending silent messages of a happier future. Suddenly his mouth descended, teasing hers with leashed passion. Invading the moist warmth of her mouth, he sent a bursting heat through her lower limbs, making her weak and dizzy. His arms tightened, holding her so close she could feel his heartbeat against her breast. It felt good, right. Then, suddenly, a dark invading panic overwhelmed her and she began to fight, dragging his arms away and pushing against his chest.

"No, don't. Please!"

He smothered a groan and stepped back, his chest still

heaving. "I'm sorry. I scared you, didn't I?" Noah reached for a glass and turned on the tap for water, not looking at her until he drank it down. "Tell me something, Dianna. Is it me or a bad memory?" he asked quietly.

"I—I don't know. Sometimes it's Charles."

"And the other times?"

"I don't know."

He sighed heavily. "Never mind. We'll work it out in time."

Dianna turned and walked slowly through the living room and out to the patio. The lights of the city twinkled below, making Dallas look like a brightly lit Christmas tree. The sounds of traffic wafted through the air, but she didn't hear them. She was wondering if she and Noah would ever really work it out.

Tabby was scheduled to enter the hospital on Thursday afternoon. Wednesday morning Tabby and Dianna dressed in time to have breakfast with Noah. The child was in love with the idea of having a family and was constantly giving both of them instructions on what and what not to do, for as far as she was concerned, she was the only person in their threesome who knew just how a family should be run.

After they saw Noah off to work, it was time to go shopping for Tabby's clothing. Tabby was so thrilled to be able to walk into Neiman-Marcus and pay for clothing with Noah's small rectangular piece of plastic that Dianna received as much satisfaction from watching her reactions as she did from the relief of not having to worry about the cost or copying the styles to sew them at home. They bought jeans in blue, yellow, tan, and green. New tops were selected—some with pastel satin flowers to match her bright colored jeans. Sneakers and shoes were purchased—then came the underwear and new dresses for her first term in school. Dianna had never seen Tabby so excited before and was torn between concern for her health and gratitude to Noah. It was he who had planned this shopping expedition so that Tabby would have her new clothes to look forward to after the operation.

After shopping all morning, they returned to the apartment just in time for lunch with Noah. Dianna wasn't sure how he knew they were back, but within minutes of their arrival Noah was there, listening to Tabby's stories of the funny and pretty things she had seen and bought. But the morning's shopping had taken its toll and Tabby was quiet during lunch itself. Her thin cheeks wore red banners and her eyelids drooped with weariness as she ate the food placed in front of her.

Directly after eating Tabby went into her room for a nap while Dianna and Noah spent an hour or so just relaxing on the patio with coffee and easy, sporadic conversation. Dianna still felt shy with him, but during the afternoon they both made headway in learning each other's likes and dislikes, thoughts and feelings. His easy, relaxed manner helped break down the barriors that she had put up between them to protect herself. He had not taken her into the master bedroom since their wedding night and she sensed a tenseness about him, as if he was waiting for her to give him some sort of signal. As much as she wanted him, she just couldn't do it—yet. However, she knew the time was approaching and it heightened the already electric atmosphere between them. She remembered the light feathery touch of his hands, his slow, drugging kisses that wiped away everything but the thought of belonging to him. During those moments together on the patio vivid images of their lovemaking flashed through her mind and she held her breath. Noah seemed to read her thoughts, but still he waited for her to make the next move. She could see it in his eyes, feel it in the controlled intimacy of his kiss as he left her to return to the office.

7

Thursday, the day Tabby was scheduled to enter the hospital, dawned clear and hot—another scorching Texas summer morning. The sun was heating the living room before breakfast and the patio doors were already closed to give the air conditioning a chance to work. For Dianna, who had never had money to buy more than one small window unit for Tabby's room, the refreshing coolness in the penthouse was an unheard-of luxury.

Tabby dressed quickly and was knocking on the bathroom door as Noah shaved and Dianna straightened their three bedrooms. He stood over the bathroom sink with chest bared and a pair of tight-fitting black slacks hugging his muscled thighs, wielding an old-fashioned shaving brush as he hummed a popular song.

He grinned at Tabby as she peered around the corner of the door, braids neatly hanging on both sides to touch the waistband of her new green jeans. "Did you come to watch or give me lessons?"

Tabby giggled as she skipped to the counter and perched herself next to his shaving equipment. "Do you always have to do this?" she asked, wonder in her little girl voice as she watched him hide behind the white foamy lather.

"Always." He nodded. "Unless you'd like me to grow a beard?"

"Ugh, no! Men with beards look mean!"

He leaned toward her and pulled a face. She laughed delightedly before running a finger down the side of his cheek and placing the foam on the tip of his nose. "It looks like the topping Mommy puts on my pudding!"

Dianna listened to the banter between the two of them as she slipped the bedspread over the pillow in Noah's room. There was a warmth, an invisible rapport between them that seemed stronger with every passing day. She was glad she had called a truce between herself and Noah. It had made all the difference in the world in Tabby's attitude. Thanks to Noah, Tabby had everything to look forward to. She no longer seemed to be at all hesitant about the operation. She had even wanted to enter the hospital early today so she could get well faster and live on the ranch quicker! Dianna glanced toward the open bathroom door to watch Tabby staring intently at Noah as he shaved.

Mrs. Frank gave a call for breakfast and Dianna stepped to the door to relay the message, only to halt, unobserved. Noah was scraping the razor down his face as Tabby, head tilted, watched with fascination. When he was finished he took the towel and wiped the remaining lather from his face, looking clean shaven and . . . very male. He slapped on after-shave, then turned to help Tabby down, holding her in midair for just the time it took to plant a quick kiss on the tip of her nose. Dianna's heart turned over, the resemblance between the two striking her forcibly. Her mind balked at the thought.

"Hey, you two! Breakfast."

"Coming." Noah reached for his shirt and began dressing as he entered the bedroom behind Tabby. He smiled slowly at Dianna, taking in her dark blue dress and white, low-heeled shoes. The outfit was crisp and neat-looking, but lacked the polished sophistication of a Neiman-Marcus ensemble.

"All that shopping and no new dress for your mother?"

"I told her to buy some with that plastic card, but she said no."

"Perhaps while you're in the hospital I'll take her shopping."

"Good idea. After all, she ought to look as pretty as *I* do." Tabby looked down in admiration at her new satin-trimmed blouse, only to look up again in confusion when both adults burst into laughter. What was so funny about looking good?

Mrs. Frank's voice could be heard from the open kitchen door and Tabby's eyes lit with expectation. "Mrs. Frank promised to make French toast this morning!" She whooped in delight, scooting out the door and down the hallway, completely ignoring her mother's protests concerning running.

Dianna turned and reached for her watch, which she had removed before doing her household chores. She didn't want to acknowledge Noah's presence directly behind her but knew he was buttoning his shirt with deft fingers. Her own were suddenly all thumbs as she tried to fasten the clasp of her watch with one hand. His warm breath fell softly on her neck.

"And how is Mrs. Weston this morning?" he murmured huskily.

She gave a shaky laugh as she turned to face him, holding out her wrist. "Nervous. Can you do this for me?"

His touch sent tingles up her arm as he bent over her hand, a frown on his brow. "When did you get this relic?"

"It was a high school graduation present from my parents." Her eyes focused on his dark springy hair, clean and still glistening from his shower. He was so distinguished, so handsome. . . .

He looked up, smiling boyishly. "My, that really dates you. I'd have guessed that marvelous antique piece at thirty years if a day—until I look at the owner." His hand held hers in a warm clasp, bringing it to his chest. "Don't I even get a reward for being Johnny-on-the-spot?"

"Is your name Johnny?" she teased, excited by his nearness.

"No, but I'm damn well on the spot." His mouth was so close to hers. All she had to do was stand on tiptoe and she could touch his lips with hers. He waited, his eyes inquiring if she had enough nerve to carry through. Slowly, slowly, she stood on tiptoe and placed her mouth on his. His arms encircled her waist, pulling her so close she could feel his hard male outline. He didn't move until she tried to pull away, then his grasp tightened and his lips opened invitingly.

Dianna stiffened for only a second before giving in to his touch. His other hand came down to claim the curve of her hip as he moved suggestively against her, making sure she understood his unspoken question. Her blood soared with unbidden memories of his body close to hers, doing wonderfully demanding things that blocked out everything except him.

Her arms crept around Noah's neck, pulling him closer, then traveled down his back and over his muscled shoulders to his chest. She unbuttoned the soft silk shirt to splay her fingers in the dark curly mat of hair. Her body molded closer in sweet intensity, and yet it was not enough. She was doing the leading now—pressing, touching, moving, feeling. A moan escaped her throat to be answered by his own as one hand curled around the swelling softness of her breast. Nothing mattered, nothing except Noah. His hands left the firm swell of her hips only to entwine about her waist to pull her still closer. She arched her back to accommodate him, loving the feeling of being held against him and wishing their clothing wasn't a barrier. Then all thought was obliterated as her need for him escalated to wanton passion.

"Hey, Mommy, you're going to get cold French toast if you don't hurry. Do you guys have to kiss so long?" Tabby stood in the bedroom doorway, a quizzical expression on her face as she watched with apparent interest. Dianna buried her head in Noah's shoulder, unable to face her daughter.

"We'll be right there, Kitten. Keep Mrs. Frank company." Noah's voice was husky, his breath coming quickly as he watched Tabby leave. "You can come out now, Di. She's gone." He was looking down at her with a hint of laughter in his eyes. "Do you have an invisible button on you somewhere that you push when you can't cope anymore?"

"If I did, I forgot to push it." She took a step back, unable to look at him, but his arm tightened, his hand continuing to tantalize her back.

"Every time I think it's the beginning, it becomes the end," he stated wryly. "But someday there will be no reprieve. Think you can handle it?"

Her head was bent, her own breathing slowing along with his. "Does it matter?"

"Dammit, of course it matters! I want you to want me as much as I want you! I'm not some kind of sex maniac that has to have you under *any* conditions!" He silently cursed himself for his bluntness before continuing in a softer voice. "I want the pleasure to be mutual."

"Noah?" she asked hesitantly, not daring to look directly at his face. Instead she played with a button on his shirt until his hand stilled hers, his thumb caressing her palm to send warm bursts of feeling through her. "Why are you so kind to—us? To me?" She glanced up through her lashes and then down at his hand again.

"Can't you figure it out?" He studied her closely.

"Is it because, because you want me?"

"Yes." His voice was quiet, but she could feel the deep rumbling of that single word beneath her hand. It seemed to vibrate through her body. "I want you in the dark warmth of night and in the cold light of day. I want you when I'm riding in an elevator, sipping a cup of coffee, standing in a crowded room. Yes. I want you."

She turned slowly, walking out of his arms and toward

the door, her back ramrod straight. He didn't try to restrain her, his hands falling away to relax at his sides as he silently stood where she had left him.

That was it. He wanted her. And instead of happiness, the knowledge brought a cold, lonely sadness to her heart.

The early morning sunlight made long narrow shadows of the tall buildings that formed the Dallas skyline. Dianna had left Noah discussing Catherine Sinclair's upcoming trial with Philip on the telephone in his study. She had met Jimmy, the chauffeur, in the lobby and asked him to take her to the hospital. It was barely seven o'clock when she reached the room where she'd left Tabby the night before, but Tabby had already been readied for surgery and given a sedative. A plump nurse with kind, smiling eyes had then directed her to the waiting room. Now she stood facing the window, her back to the antiseptic green-and-white walls that left her more depressed than before. It didn't really matter, she thought. Nothing mattered anymore. Noah, Catherine, June, the mess her life had become. Nothing. The only reality was Tabby and the desperate hope that she was strong enough to pull through the operation. Dianna crossed her arms and began her ritual pacing, stopping occasionally to stare out at the view she had not yet been able to consciously register in her mind's eye.

Tabby had looked so lost when the orderlies came to wheel her into surgery. Her little arms were so thin; her long caramel-colored hair was bundled into a white paper cap, making her look even tinier than she was. Her features were so wan, so drawn. Her tiny body so lifeless . . .

A sob rose in her throat and she covered her face with trembling hands as tears trickled between her fingers. Loneliness isolated her from everyone. She was alone. There was no one with whom to share her heartache, her doubts, her aching emptiness. Why? Why was she being punished for something she didn't do? Why was Tabby suffering for being the sweet child she was? It made no sense! Her eyes lifted, searching the dusty white ceiling for heaven. Her lips moved in silent prayer. "Please, God, let her live! Please, God! Please!"

Life without Tabby? There was none. Once again she buried her head in her hands, unable to bear the pain that seemed to squeeze the blood from her heart. Suddenly there were strong gentle arms around her, holding her tenderly but firmly in their grasp. She didn't look up, uncaring for the moment whose broad shoulder she was using. She was content to be consoled as hands stroked her hair, rocking her slightly against a hard chest. Giant sobs racked her body as she tried to gulp for air until finally there were no more tears, just a feeling of washed-out peace. A handkerchief was placed in her trembling fingers.

"I'm sorry I wasn't here sooner." Noah's voice was warm, his breath soft against her throbbing temple. He continued to hold her as she wiped her eyes and blew her reddened nose. Nothing ladylike about me now, she thought.

"I didn't expect you here at all."

He took the handkerchief from her hands and dabbed lightly at the smeared mascara under her eyes, smiling tenderly at her bewilderment. "Tabby's my daughter too now. Did you think I'd let you go through this alone?"

"Tabby's only been your daughter for a week. I've

been alone for the past six years, Noah. I didn't expect it to be any different now." She wasn't speaking with anger or bitterness, just resignation. How could she expect him to care for a child he hardly knew?

"Waiting is the hardest thing to do alone. Especially when it involves someone you love."

"How did you know?"

"My sister was in this same hospital seven years ago with a stroke." His voice was void of emotion, but she could feel the tension in his arms. Then his tone turned brisk. "And that ended very well, too. She's completely recovered." He grinned. "How about a cup of coffee? Mrs. Frank packed a thermos full. She says she doesn't want my missus trying to drink that ink that comes out of a machine." Dianna smiled as he'd meant her to. "Now why don't you have a seat, Mrs. Weston?"

They sat quietly side by side for a while. Dianna barely noticed how hard she clung to the hand that covered hers. It felt good to hang on, hang on.

He began talking of mundane things: the weather, the ranch, his work, her work. At first she answered abstractedly, her mind hardly able to cope with his questions, but the more he forced her to answer, the more she began to relax.

"Why did you decide to keep Tabby?" he asked suddenly.

"Because Tabby's mine!" she retorted quickly, surprising herself with the answer.

"You had plenty of other options, yet you chose to keep her. Why?"

She tried hard to remember back to that difficult time in her life. "I'm not sure, really. I was brought up with strong religious beliefs and I knew I couldn't live with an abortion. Then, when it came to the question of giving her away, I couldn't do that either. Somehow I thought I would never marry and this would be my one chance at motherhood. I would be able to raise a child—my child—and give it all the love and understanding I could."

"And you'd never be lonely again," he added softly.

"That wasn't my intent!"

"Come on, Dianna. None of us gives without wanting something in return. Even love."

"What do you know about love!" she snapped. "All you know how to do is go through the motions."

"Sometimes that's enough." She hated his smile, hated his cock-sure self-confidence. Who did he think he was to enter into her life and begin analyzing her motives?

"And don't tell me you don't like the motions, Di," he went on. "My memory isn't that short. I still remember what it feels like to have you come alive in my arms."

Her face burned with the knowledge of those sweet nights years ago. "You don't have to remind me of past mistakes."

Noah's eyebrow quirked but his expression remained impassive. "Was that what it was? A mistake? Is that why you've hung on to the memory of Charles and blocked out our passion? Is it easier to hate him than love me?"

"Stop it!" She jumped up, only to come face to face with Dr. Storn. Once again every fiber of her being was focused on Tabby. He related the details of the operation and its success with a kind smile, quickly easing the worried look that had come over her features.

"By the way, Mr. Weston, her last words were 'I want a red pony with a star on its forehead like the picture.' Her attitude is so good that I expect to see her playing tennis in a day or so just to get into shape for riding that pony she's been promised!" He laughed, shaking his head in disbelief. "I wish all my patients had something like that to lure them out of their sickbeds. Attitude is the only ingredient that I can't control, yet it makes all the difference in the world."

Noah nodded his head, ignoring Dianna's surprise. "When can we see her?"

"You can see her now if you only stay a minute or two." His eyes softened as they rested on Dianna. "She won't know you yet, you realize."

"We understand," Noah interjected smoothly. "I think my wife just wants to assure herself of Tabby's recovery, then I'll take her home to rest."

"Oh, but I'm staying here!" Dianna exclaimed.

The doctor shook his head. "No buts about it, young lady. You won't be able to see Tabby again until tomorrow morning at the earliest. You ought to do what your husband suggests. If Tabby sees you tired and washed out tomorrow then she'll be worried, and that will impede her progress." His tone was kindly but brooked no argument.

She should have been angry with them for making her decisions for her, but she wasn't. It was a nice feeling to have the two men take the responsibility out of her hands. She followed them quietly down the hall, content to let them carry the conversation. All she wanted was to see Tabby. Secretly, Dianna was more tired than she would admit.

* * *

The powerful car ate up the pavement as it headed toward home and Dianna drifted off to sleep under the spell of the engine's lullabye. She awoke with a start when the movement of the car stilled and the comforting hum of the engine abruptly stopped. Dianna pulled herself up, her hazel eyes growing wide with surprise although she was still half asleep. Her senses were not sharp, but even half asleep Dianna knew she wasn't home yet. With a feeling of foreboding she turned toward Noah. He was watching her carefully.

"Where are we?"

"We're home."

"No. *No!*" She glanced around for the first time, confirming her fears. They were in the basement of Wescomp and in every corner lurked ghosts ready to remind her of things better left in the past.

8

◦◦◦◦◦◦◦◦◦◦◦

Fear made the pupils of her eyes seem like hazel pools. She began trembling even more. Noah's piercing gray gaze caught hers, silently sending her his strength and willing her to fight the debilitating fear.

"Is the idea of being home so abhorrent to you?" he said gently, a half-teasing note in his low voice.

Dianna shook her head. "It's this, this . . ."

"You haven't been down here since the party, have you?"

"Jimmy picks me up at the lobby entrance," she stammered, her gaze sweeping every corner of the darkened lot as her fingernails dug into the flesh of her arms.

He held her against his broad chest, smoothing back a curling tendril of ebony-colored hair. Her eyes were wide, looking even larger than usual in her pale face. She could feel his steady heartbeat as his hands ran over her back in an attempt to infuse her with some of his strength.

"Look around you, Dianna. There's nothing here to frighten you. There's only good lighting, security guards, bright colors, and lots of cars. Nothing else. It's just a building. That's all." He tried to soothe her, but his words could not penetrate the barrier of fear around her heart. He gave a deep sigh. "It seems the only way to erase old memories is to give you new ones to think about."

She knew what he was going to do but couldn't move to avoid it. He was casting a spell: old and new, new and old. Old ghosts fought with the new feelings that flooded her body. She watched, mesmerized, as Noah's mouth descended upon hers, sweeping her into a vortex of heated emotions. The warmth in her blood flowed quickly to ease the shaking that had begun with her realization of where she was. Now she was conscious of neither time nor place, aware only of the world inside the car, with Noah.

She was no longer frightened. Butterflies swirled in her stomach and her hands became moist as they clutched Noah's silky shirt. Pulling or pushing? She didn't know. The flat of his hands moved sensuously across her back, molding her to him intimately, leaving a burning heat where they touched. His lips were warm, moist, firm, against hers, teaching her to respond to him all over again. Slowly she understood the depth of his wanting and realized that her own desire matched it. She wanted him to stay with her, hold her, keep the dark underworld of the basement at bay. And he did. Her heart beat faster, no longer in fear but in need. Then his hands were everywhere, softly, softly, molding, melting. Butterfly wings unfurled to send out radiating heat through her slender form and with a wild abandon she pulled him closer, unsatisfied with their separateness. All thought, all inhibition was lost. It was just the two of them, and nothing else mattered.

"That you, Mr. Weston?" A man's gravelly voice stopped Dianna's heart for a beat. She glanced over Noah's shoulder to see the guard as he tapped on the window, a knowing look in his eyes.

"Yes, Watts, it's me." Noah's eyes registered the heightened color on Dianna's high cheekbones. "Everything all right?"

"Yes, sir. Everything's just fine." He turned and continued his stroll through the parked cars, leaving Dianna still breathless and slightly confused.

His deep gray-black eyes twinkled at her, a small smile playing about his mouth. "Not only do I break my promise to leave you alone, but I also get caught at it!" Noah chuckled without a trace of remorse and Dianna pushed herself away from his broad chest. The further away from him she was, the better she could think!

"It's just as well. I don't think this is the right time to pursue what you had in mind—or the right place!" She realized what she had said and turned dismayed eyes to him. "I'm sorry. I wasn't trying to . . . to . . ."

He sighed heavily. "I know, I know. The whole Weston clan is to blame for what happened to you here." He took a breath, then gave her a slow, warm smile. "At least your response wasn't forced!" he teased before getting out to help her from her side of the car. He guided her to the elevator and pushed the button. "Hope springs eternal," he murmured, glancing at her bowed head as she strove for an inner calmness that would not come.

How could she have been so reckless? How could he be so controlled now when just a few minutes ago they had both been like animals in heat, panting in unison? Another flush covered her cheeks and she deliberately kept her face averted from him. He was only trying to make the best of a bad situation that he had been forced into, just as she was. That was all.

As they stepped off the elevator a distant beat of music drifted through the hallway. Surprised, Dianna glanced at the guard lounging against the wall.

"Afternoon," he mumbled, straightening instantly when he saw Noah.

"Where's the music coming from?" she asked, knowing the answer almost immediately as she followed Noah's eyes down the darkened corridor. At the end, a door stood partially open and a streak of light illuminated the hallway, the music coming from the room beyond. Noah's grip tightened as he led her toward their door, but she stopped, waiting for his answer.

"I thought you knew. There are two suites on this floor. Ours and the one that originally belonged to Charles."

She placed her purse on the hall table as they entered the apartment. "Is that where you put Catherine?" She straightened, turning to face him, but he was gone. The study door clicked softly closed.

She was almost glad he hadn't heard her question. She

didn't want to know the answer. If he told her yes she would be forced to respond with heated indignation, and if he said no she wouldn't believe him anyway. Such logic! She walked into her bedroom and slipped out of her shoes. The bed was soft and inviting, the silk coverlet feeling cool and soothing. Why wasn't she angry? Her tired brain couldn't come up with an answer. She would worry about one thing at a time, and right now her main worry should be Tabby.

Her last thoughts were of what would have happened if the guard in the parking lot had not interrupted. Letting herself imagine the possibilities, she was surprised to find she was not the least irritated with the idea. In fact . . .

She didn't know what time she woke up, but the lights of the city were now reflected in the ceiling of the dark and cloudy sky. She stretched, feeling wonderfully refreshed and very hungry. As if to prove that she needed food, her stomach growled, making her smile.

The hall light was on, as was a lamp in the living room, but there was no Noah. She entered the kitchen and began cooking at once, quickly sautéing several ingredients together in a pan before finding the bacon and eggs. Once the bacon was done, she poured the eggs in and began her omelet. She hummed softly, so intent on what she was doing that she didn't hear the door swing open.

"Looks like you're making enough to feed the entire office staff!" Noah grinned before bending to place a kiss lightly on her ear. "Will there be enough for me to have a bite?"

"Of course. *If* you like onions, tomatoes, mushrooms, cheese, and bacon in your omelet." Her smile came quickly, a natural response to his lighthearted mood.

"Good grief!" He moaned in mock horror. "I've heard of omelets with any one of those ingredients, but never all!"

"Then you haven't lived." She grated a small amount of cheese. "Sometimes we have omelets for dinner when I've had a bad day and don't really feel like cooking. Tabby loves this combination."

"With such a notable authority giving her approval, how could I possibly turn it down?" He rummaged in the drawer for silverware and set the table, picking up the tune Dianna had been humming and harmonizing with her own notes.

Dianna's heart soared and she pushed the thoughts of yesterday and tomorrow out of her mind. She was determined not to break the peace that had finally come over the two of them. It was a fine thread with which to build a tapestry of life, but everything had to start somewhere.

Noah made her wish she had invented something special for their late snack as he applauded her efforts. They cleaned the kitchen together, leaving it spotless enough even for Mrs. Frank. After a fleeting hesitation, she gave in to the pressure of his arm around her shoulders as he guided her from the kitchen to the master bedroom. He continued to hum the wordless tune as they entered the darkened room, but despite it, easiness fled. They both knew what he was leading up to and she wasn't prepared to deal with it. Not yet.

"I think I'll take a shower," she managed as she drew away from him and moved toward the bathroom.

He looked surprised but amused. "I must have the cleanest wife in town," he murmured as he leaned over the bed and pushed a switch Dianna had not yet investigated. Soft, dreamy music filled the air to make the surroundings more intimate, and as Dianna hesitated by the bathroom door she realized the bedroom now made the perfect setting for a seduction. The lights were lowered just enough to form shadows in the corners, shining gently on the large satin-sheeted bed. Thoughts of the same place but in another time flitted through her mind, reminding her of Noah's gentle lovemaking, and her cheeks blushed becomingly.

Noah lay with his hands beneath his head, his back propped up by the headboard. His legs were crossed and his dark gray knowing eyes held a smoky look. His shirt gaped open to show a shadow of dark springy curls on his broad chest. She crossed to the bathroom and closed the door quickly, wondering if she was using it as a barrier to him—or herself.

The shower stall was large and completely tiled in oatmeal-colored ceramic. The water was hot and inviting, soothing her tense muscles. Strangely enough, tonight they were not half as tight as they had been in nights past. She let her head drop forward as the water gently massaged her neck. She tried to avoid the mental picture of Noah as she had left him, relaxed, yet with sexual magnetism emanating from every pore. No man should have that much sensuality!

Suddenly the shower door opened and Dianna turned quickly, only to lose her balance on the slick soapy floor. Noah steadied her with a hand on her waist as he calmly stepped in and shut the door behind him.

"Easy there, darling." His voice echoed against the walls, surrounding her with its velvety roughness.

"What are you doing here?" She turned, refusing to let

him see the blush that spread over her cheeks as his nearness sent her into confusion.

"Since Mohammed won't come to the mountain . . ." he teased as his hand glided down her waist to rest on the swell of her hip. His other hand reached for the soap and began lathering her neck. It was a caressing touch as the soap bar circled slowly downward around the tips of her upturned breasts then moved lazily between them to descend toward her flat, taut stomach. They stood a foot apart, but Dianna felt as if he was on top of her, hardly allowing her breathing space. Yet a hungry, yearning desire slowly unfurled deep inside her, like a night blossom in the early dusk. She watched his soapy hands as they formed a pattern. She couldn't tear her eyes away from them.

"I've already soaped," she protested weakly, unable to say it with any conviction. But he wasn't looking at her, he was looking at her pointed nipples, watching them peak and turn harder with every motion of the soap in his hand.

"Please, I . . ."

"Turn around," he commanded hoarsely, and she obeyed, waiting for whatever might happen. The soap traveled down her back in a zigzag motion, slowly moving toward her waist and buttocks. The water continued to rain down on their wet, glistening bodies as he changed the shower head to a rythmic pulsing throb, turning Dianna so it sprayed her breasts with the sensation of long, teasing fingers. He continued to lather her hips, then let his hand move around so the hard tips of his fingers could stroke her stomach. She couldn't move; the languorous feeling that spread through her body like liquid mercury made her limbs too weak. She had never known feelings so intense before. Sensation after sensation washed over her. He was hypnotizing her into wanting him and it was too delicious to stop. When she swayed, his hands pulled her to rest against his chest and she could feel his masculine need for her. His breath was as ragged as her own, ruffling the hair at her temple. He was blotting out all the hurt, all the bad memories she had harbored so long. There was only now, here, with him.

"Your skin is like smooth silk." His hips moved slowly back and forth and the sensation was so good she mindlessly responded with thrusts of her own.

"Oh, Dianna." He gave a shuddering groan, trying to maintain some control over himself, stilling the motions of love. "Wait, darling. Wait." His hand continued to soothe and stroke.

She sighed in response, resting her head in the hollow of his shoulder.

Noah turned her to face him, bending down to take one rosy-tipped breast in his mouth and suck gently. From far away she heard a feline purr and realized it was her own. Her hands came down of their own accord and cradled him, caressing his strong, lean body in a haze of desire, reveling in the blatant power of the muscles beneath her fingertips. Before she knew what he was doing, they were out of the shower and dripping across the bathroom floor to the closed commode seat, where he slipped her around to straddle him. Her eyes were closed as she reveled in the sensation of his magic touch, his wet and slippery body.

He took the pins from her hair, dropping them to the

floor, and fluffed the dampened tendrils around her shoulders, murmuring against her breast. She arched her body, reflexes following his directions, his movements, as he rocked her to and fro in a rhythm meant only for lovers. Stars and vibrant colors burst in a spiral of feeling as fire exploded inside her. Their gasps mingled as he thrust himself still deeper to make the heights of their ecstacy complete.

Finally they began to descend gently together, holding each other tightly as they caught their breath and rested. Skin to skin, forehead to forehead, they were as one, his hands stroking her back as he softly murmured love names.

She was so dazed from such a flood of feeling that she hardly noticed when Noah picked her up and, cradling her in his arms as he carried her effortlessly to the bed, placed her gently on the satin coverlet. Seconds later he was there with a towel, drying her soft, damp body. She loved the tamed strength of his hands, his soothing massaging motions with the roughness of the terry cloth. Soon the towel was gone and he slipped into bed, holding her in the crook of his arm as he sighed contentedly. She felt his kiss against her temple, then sleep came to hold her close and she felt nothing—nothing but peace.

The cover weighed heavily around her waist and she tried to tug it up before she realized it was a well-muscled arm that kept her gently pinned in the soft, comfortable bed. She eased slowly to her other side, not wanting him to waken.

Noah was sleeping. He looked much like a small boy.

now, his face uncreased, his breath steady and deep. Why was she feeling no shame at her behavior earlier? Why was she so comforted by his arm holding her close?

She had lived another day and in that day nothing she had done could be changed, redone, rethought. It had happened and would change all the tomorrows, but not the yesterdays. She couldn't go back, and with that thought another came close on its heels. She did not want to go back. It was good having someone to take care of her, watch out for her, help and love her. She closed her eyes and went back to sleep, her mouth curving in a small secret smile.

A feathered kiss fluttered against her forehead, another, then another. A deep chuckle echoed close to her ear as a hand caressed bare shoulders, then moved down to claim her breast, cupping it as if to decide its weight. Startled, Dianna opened her eyes, and the whole scope of her vision was filled with Noah's face. Her eyes glowed with instant memories of the night before and he knew it, could read it in her expression.

"Well, Mrs. Weston. We'd better get ready to see our daughter." He quirked one dark eyebrow, a small grin lighting his face. "Unless you wouldn't mind staying in bed a little while longer?" he added suggestively, forcing Dianna to look away in confusion. Her eyes darted over his bare chest, strong arms, corded neck, and the same heightened emotions that had flowed through her last night returned with even more force.

"What time is it?" She didn't want to acknowledge his invitation but was equally unable to refuse.

"Time enough for what I have in mind," he muttered before covering her mouth with a kiss meant to devour all sweetness. Wrapping her arms around his waist, she reveled in the feeling of his coarse chest hair against her breasts. Reality disappeared as a sensuous warmth wove its way through her body.

They saw Tabby again that morning and Dianna was amazed by her alertness. Thanks to modern painkillers, she was resting comfortably and her bright eyes examined the room and her parents with interest. Her smile was shy for the first moment or so, then she relaxed, asking Noah a hundred questions about her pony and the ranch. Tabby's only worry, as her head began to finally nod in sleep, was that she would not be able to see her favorite TV program later in the afternoon. After consulting with the nurse, Noah promised a television would be brought in later in the day, and they would be back to watch it with her.

After leaving the hospital, they walked the downtown streets holding hands and ducking into doorways to steal a kiss, finally not even caring for privacy and kissing on the sidewalk. They made nonsense noises and said nonsense words, just like children skipping school and finding the release heady. Their composed, secretive selves had disappeared to leave two exuberant, uninhibited lovers that neither had ever known existed in the other.

They smiled at grim faces and harried strangers. They ate tacos in a small luncheonette. They held hands and shared the same large Coke. Dianna spilled taco sauce on the front of her blouse and Noah, laughing, grabbed a napkin and began cleaning it up as if she were a child. But the laughter died in his throat as his hands touched her breast. They stared silently at each other, both acknowledging the intense hunger they saw in one another's eyes.

He led her down the block to the Fairmont Hotel and strolled up to the marble desk, arrogantly requesting a room. They were given one without question and he marched her toward the elevator, the twinkle of mischief in his eyes belying his straight face.

"What are we doing here?" she whispered.

"Pretending we're not married."

She nodded her head toward the desk. "Do they think that?"

"Of course. People will think anything if you act the part."

"Are we acting the part?"

"Do we have luggage?" He grinned and she giggled, seeing the situation through the desk clerk's experienced eyes.

The room was big, the bed almost sinfully wide. They were on the twelfth floor and the view of downtown Dallas was breathtaking. The Texas sky was a pale heated blue, the July sun hot on the window glass. Dianna loved it. She hugged herself.

"I feel very, very wicked."

"And you will be—soon." He leered, and she laughed.

Noah picked up the phone and ordered a bottle of champagne, then came up behind her and put his arms around her waist, his chin resting on the top of her head. They both looked out the window, neither seeing the view as they felt the heartbeating nearness of the other. When the bellhop's knock sounded though the room Noah reluctantly answered it, giving the young boy an extravagant tip before taking the tray of champagne and glasses and shutting the door with a definite slam. He opened the bottle and poured two glasses, handing one to Dianna.

He looked down at her as she sipped her drink, the bubbles making her nose tickle.

"May all your honeymoons be filled with me."

She glanced up and their eyes locked, her merriment disappearing under the glow of his smoky eyes. He placed his glass on the table and slowly began unbuttoning her blouse. She held her glass to one side and watched his deft fingers, feeling a detached sort of wicked excitement at what he was doing. His hands sought and found the clasp to her skirt and unzipped it before taking the glass from her hand and holding it to her lips for one last sip before he placed it next to his.

When panties and bra were removed he stripped his own clothing off, watching her gaze at him in fascination. Soon they were both naked in the sunlit room, standing less than a foot apart.

"Welcome to Noah Weston's School in the Art of Love."

"Is that what this is? I don't see any art."

"I do." His eyes glittered with meaning as his glance swept over her body. He lifted the champagne bottle and tilted it to trickle liquid between her breasts, making a wet trail down to her navel, then further. She watched, one part of her mind wondering why she was allowing him to do this, while the other accepted it all with intense excitement. His dark head bent to kiss the liquid away. He gave her more to drink as he touched her here and touched her there, never actually taking her in his arms.

Her body responded, craving for him to do something to ease the heated aching he had awakened. Still he did nothing.

"Noah, please," she whispered. Her head was spinning, yet he held up the glass for her to take another sip.

"Noah, please what?"

"Don't do this."

His fingers found the moist core of her desire, then moved up to stroke her already tautened belly. "Don't do what? This? Or this?" He smiled and she could see the triumph lurking there.

"Don't tease me."

"Teasing you wasn't what I had in mind. I just want you to be ready enough to do what I say." Desire was in his eyes, but there was also a thread of determination there.

Her look answered him more clearly than a shout.

He led her to the bed, throwing back the covers and placing her diagonally across it. She was on her back with her eyes closed, feet dangling as he stood between her legs, letting glistening drops of champagne fall upon her. She watched, afraid to move, to stop him. Her body was beyond her control, calling out for relief. Suddenly he was on his knees, his mouth like liquid fire, his tongue seeking, searching, urging her on. Dianna couldn't tell him to stop. She was swept away by the passionate feelings he evoked deep inside her. When his body moved over hers and he filled her with himself she burst with passion as they both sought the ultimate union—to become one for just a fleeting moment in time. Moans mingled with moans, breathing with breathing, before they were totally meshed together.

"My wife. My Dianna," he murmured into the softness

of her neck as they both drifted down from the mountainous heights together.

They checked out of the room and caught a taxi back to the hospital in time to watch Tabby's program with her. The little girl nodded through most of it, asking few questions as tiredness overwhelmed her. Over her head Noah's eyes locked with Dianna's, a becoming blush spreading across her cheeks to be answered by a small tender smile on Noah's face. It was as if they communicated without speaking. What had happened between them to so drastically change their personalities? Dianna didn't want to know. She didn't want to think. Everything had changed in the space of twenty-four hours and she never wanted to go back to the time before. A new Dianna was emerging, and even though she liked this new self, she was also slightly scared. Would nothing ever be the same?

They left Tabby sleeping, telling the nurse they would be back in the morning to spend the day. Jimmy was parked by the hospital door. He glanced at them occasionally on the way back to the apartment, but apart from an occasional self-satisfied smile, he never gave any indication that he noticed the difference in them.

Mrs. Frank had dinner prepared and they ate at a leisurely pace, enjoying the silence softened by slow, easy music filtering in from the stereo system in the living room. They sipped Tia Maria on the darkened patio, Dianna exclaiming over the clear night and the blanket of stars overhead. They made love and fell asleep in each other's arms, content.

9

I have a bottle of wine stashed away in the file cabinet, some pepperoni pizza on its way, and my secretary has orders to put everything on hold for the next two hours." Noah's voice was low and teasing. "I expect you down here in five minutes, woman."

Dianna laughed, a bubbly sound that echoed through her throat and came out in happy notes. "How did you know I was home?"

"I have my ways," he replied with exaggerated mystery.

She dressed quickly, throwing her slacks set on the floor in her hurry. She picked a soft cream jersey dress

Noah had chosen for her yesterday, when they had made a detour from the hospital to home. He had taken her to Neiman-Marcus and led her toward the upper-floor couturier department to drive the already tired saleswoman to distraction. He had flicked through the designer dresses himself, looking for one he obviously had in mind, until he found it. When he offered to buy more, Dianna had balked, not wanting to be bought with clothing or trinkets. Somehow Noah had understood her hesitancy and had not insisted.

He welcomed her into the office with a glass of burgundy and a comical leer, his obvious good humor making her happier than she could have believed.

"I love your dress."

"Is that a compliment to me or to you?" she teased.

"To both of us," he toasted.

They grinned at each other like two teenagers on their first date, and Dianna couldn't help wondering how many other couples had married and then begun their courtship, as they had. Had anyone else ever been as happy as she felt now?

Once the conversation began they discussed everything but themselves. Their relationship was too new yet to be dissected. The pizza was good, and after they'd eaten almost all of it, they sat back on the couch and sipped their wine. The silence, broken only by the soft music drifting from a radio in the corner cabinet, was easy. Expectation hung in the air between them. His hand rubbed the back of her neck, then softly stroked her cheek. The large glass window-wall that looked over the city was darkened to a blue-gray by an impending storm, making the room all the cozier. They were on an island by themselves. Conversation had halted completely; she couldn't keep her mind on faraway topics when her need for him was so great, and he knew it. Slowly he drew her to him, his hands knowing where to go, how to touch her. He teased her into being the aggressor and she taunted him into taking the lead back. They gave and took of each other. They made love on the carpet and it was intense, deliciously satisfying. Through the aftermath haze of lovemaking they could hear murmurings in the outside lobby and she giggled. He nuzzled her neck, breathing deeply of her softly scented skin.

"Something tells me we'll have to check into a hotel before we can get away with this again." He sighed, hearing the voices in the outer reception room.

"Better still, why not come upstairs for lunch?" She ran a manicured finger around the contour of his mouth, marveling at her own aggressiveness. Two weeks ago she would never have dreamed of doing this.

"Better still, why don't I retire and then we can do this all day?"

"All day, Mr. Weston?" she exclaimed, a mischievous glint in her eyes as she reached for her bra and panties. "Just what do you think I am?"

"Mine."

It was marvelous.

She still couldn't face how much Noah had come to mean in her life. Their relationship was too new to pick apart and examine right now. Perhaps eventually she would get used to this feeling of instant happiness whenever he was around. But not now. Now she could only marvel at it and hope . . .

Dianna was surprised at the number of things that came up to keep her busy from dawn to dusk. Yet, strangely, she was never tired from her activities, as she had been before Noah entered her life. He filled her with an inexhaustible energy that continued to grow as she used it. Mornings were spent with Tabby at the hospital—playing games, reading, watching the children's programs on television. By noon she was back home to check over the night's menu with Mrs. Frank, run a fine eye over the daily maid's cleaning, and schedule the most important chores she wanted done the next day. Noah joined her in the late afternoon and then they both visited Tabby again, staying until dark. They played Fish, Chutes and Ladders, and Spades. They laughed over Noah's mistakes but he took it all in stride, reminding them he had not learned to play games as a child and had never even had a family until two weeks ago. His looks were funny, his voice gruff, and Tabby loved him almost as much as Dianna. He was an accepted fact of life for the little girl and she adored him.

But a niggling question lurked in the back of Dianna's mind and pushed itself forward at the most inopportune times. What if Noah interfered with her raising of Tabby? Right now there was no disciplining, no schedule to be maintained—nothing but visits. But when Tabby was home and things settled into a routine, what would happen? Noah was too used to being in command not to lay down a few laws. Could they handle the problems that were bound to crop up together? She hoped so but she really wasn't sure. She had never had to share Tabby before.

Philip and his wife, Jessie, were coming to dinner and Dianna had planned the meal with special care: rack of lamb with wild rice and asparagus and for dessert *crème brûlée*. The table was set, Dianna was dressed, and their guests were at the door. There was no time to be nervous.

Five minutes after the introductions were made, Dianna was already feeling as though she and Jessie had been friends for years. The other woman was totally unlike the way Dianna had originally pictured her. She had golden red hair, a figure tending toward plump, a sense of humor that was strikingly witty in an earthy, matter-of-fact way. And she loved to argue. She didn't particularly care who was right or wrong, so long as the discussion made her think.

When dinner was over and they sat in the living room over coffee and after-dinner drinks, Dianna found herself getting caught up in just such an argument.

"Man is not an animal at all!" Jessie exclaimed, getting her point across by slapping her hand on the coffee table. "If he were, then he would have to wait until his mate was in heat to make love. Since he doesn't, I rest my case."

They laughed, Philip's eyes shining with admiration for her hard-won point. "By Jove, I think she's got something there!"

"She certainly has," Dianna interjected. "Besides, animals mate, but people make love, so there's another difference."

"It's all the same." Philip waved his hand, dismissing that argument.

"Oh, no it's not." Dianna spoke softly but with conviction, and Noah's penetrating gray eyes locked with hers, sending their own silent message.

"Amen," Noah murmured huskily, and they were suddenly the only two in the room.

"Boy, I can tell these two are still on their honeymoon!" Jessie hooted.

Noah lifted his glass toward Dianna. "Long may it last."

Jessie glanced at Philip. "And if it ends, may you have the luck to begin again." Her voice was solemn, saddened by something intangible Dianna couldn't place.

The man in the next booth smiled at her and she smiled in return before shifting slightly to make sure he understood the smile was courtesy and nothing more. She reached for her cigarettes, lighting one just as Jessie plopped down in the booth with a heaving sigh.

"Sorry I'm late. The baby-sitter didn't show up on time and then we couldn't find Beth's shoe." She pushed back her hair and gave a sigh. "What would the world do without mothers? I found it in the doghouse, slightly wet and very smelly, with one hole chewed in the toe. That dog is going to be the death of me yet. Why Phil bought that spaniel . . ." Her voice trailed off and an intense look of pain flitted across her face, but was gone before Dianna could comment. "And what is it you spend your time doing, Mrs. Weston? It's been four days since I asked you to lunch and you've been too busy every day until now."

Dianna smiled. "I see Tabby every day—sometimes twice if Noah can go with me. I check the menus, water plants, watch my nails grow . . ." Her eyes gleamed with amusement. "And then I wait for my lord and master."

"You two are still on your honeymoon. Just wait until

the glitter tarnishes." Jessie spoke bitterly, not looking at Dianna as the cocktail waitress interrupted to take their order. Dianna noticed that look of pain on Jessie's face again as she continued. "Then you wonder where the romance went, but you don't care enough to find out."

"Sounds like the 'other woman' syndrome." Dianna tried to smile, but couldn't.

"Is that so strange in this society?" Jessie asked defensively. "Let me tell you, dear heart, it's the rule rather than the exception. Just look around. I bet half the men in this restaurant are having lunch with someone other than their wives. I also bet they're paying a pretty penny for the privilege."

She paused while the young waitress set napkins on the table and placed their drinks on top of them. But when the girl had left, the silence continued, until Dianna got up enough nerve to reopen the conversation.

"Either you're a cynic or you're trying to tell me something. Which is it?" Dianna asked quietly. "Do you know something about Noah that you think you ought to tell me?"

Jessie looked up and correctly read the fear that Dianna was trying so hard to hide. Her hand reached across to rest on Dianna's, giving a slight squeeze. "Oh, no, Di. I don't mean that at all! I don't know anything new about Noah and Catherine!"

"But you're warning me against something."

"No. I just don't want you to be hurt by her."

Dianna ran her finger around the rim of her glass. "I guess you know she's living in the other suite in the penthouse."

Jessie shrugged. "It was the only place he could put

her. Anywhere else and the press would have gotten to her right away. At least up there no one can get past the security guard and make an even bigger story out of this juicy tidbit!" Jessie hesitated for a moment. "How did you know? Have you seen her?"

"It didn't take much to put two and two together."

"Have you spoken to Noah about it?"

"What do I say, Jessie? Noah, I found out that your mistress is down the hall, and I want you to either move her into your bedroom or out of our lives?" Dianna's eyes showed her anguish, emphasized by tears glistening in their hazel depths. "I know the situation sounds untenable to anyone who doesn't know the whole story, but I'm in no position to make demands."

"Nobody's in a better position than you are, as his wife, to tell him to get rid of her *now.*"

"Oh, Jessie!" Dianna fought the lump of fear in her throat as she stared into the depths of her martini. "I thought you knew that Noah only married me to take care of Tabby. He doesn't love me. We were both pushed into this marriage and are trying to make the best of it. I thought . . ." She stopped, unable to continue.

"I know. I also know that your marriage has made Noah happier than I've ever seen him. He's been lonely a long time, Dianna. Too long.

"I met him many years ago after a very unhappy love affair and we became close friends. But even then he was never happy or content. When we had dinner at your place, I thought you two had found something wonderful in each other. Phil thought so too, although he admitted he was worried when he first heard that you were married." Jessie grinned. "Phil and Noah were roommates in college and probably know each other as well as any two people can. Believe me, Catherine doesn't mean anything to Noah." Her lips thinned. "She and Charles would have made a beautiful pair, but by the time she showed up Charles was gone."

"Charles?" Dianna's voice squeaked.

Jessie glanced up in surprise before smiling ruefully. "Boy, am I the one to let family secrets out of the closet, but you might as well know. I don't think you'll tell anyone, will you? I don't want Noah to think I've been talking about him behind his back. Besides, even Noah doesn't know some of what I'm going to say, and I'd hate for him to find out this way." She smiled grimly. "The man is so closemouthed sometimes that you never know what he's thinking or if he's really an emotionless machine behind those steel-gray eyes and determined chin. For all the world knows, he may be a robot programmed for success." She laughed at her own description of Noah. "But he's really human, Dianna, and sometimes I think he's more vulnerable than the rest of us.

"Noah's younger brother, Charles, had all the advantages Noah and his older sister missed. By the time he was five their father was already gone. He died of a heart attack out in the fields. Noah found him, hours later. He was almost fifteen at the time. His mother had always been frail and the shock of her husband's death was too much for her. She passed away a few months after he did. She never had the strength to be a farmer and rancher's wife. She was too gentle, Noah always said." Jessie paused, lit a cigarette, and drew deeply, playing with the half-empty pack as she continued.

"Noah's sister raised Charles as if he were her own child. She was nineteen or twenty then, and literally gave up her youth for him, for all the good it did. Between Noah and a neighbor they kept the farm going, barely making a go of it until he graduated from high school. He won a scholarship and attended college, working at the same time. They had sold a small portion of the land by that time and were living on the invested money.

"Noah started up Wescomp to give his sister and brother the security of money. Only it didn't work that way." Jessie eyed Dianna's white face through the haze of smoke. "I know—it sounds like something out of a novel, doesn't it? But it's all true, and Charles grew up just as you'd predict. He was spoiled and expected all his demands to be met. Usually they were. Noah's sister denied him nothing. Maybe she wasn't strong enough to cope with him—I don't know. Anyway, Charles attended Baylor and was kicked out. He attended the University of Texas and was kicked out. Then he attended St. Mary's in San Antonio and got into a scrape with the law. Grades, behavior, morals: they were all listed as faults on his records.

"Noah threatened to cut off his allowance if he got into trouble one more time, and as luck would have it some young girl friend of his accused him of being the father of her child. Charles knew that Noah would not give him another penny if he found out, so he went to Philip for help. When all was said and done, Philip couldn't turn him down."

Jessie waved the waiter away, checking with Dianna quickly. Neither was ready to order.

"Anyway, it turned out that a week before Charles

151

died in that traffic accident Philip learned that Charles was sterile. Something to do with having had mumps as a child."

"Are you sure?" Dianna's ashen face made her hazel eyes stand out like two burned holes in an ivory tablecloth.

"Oh, I'm sure. Philip and I talked and talked about it. I wanted him to tell Noah, but he was adamantly against it, saying he had problems enough to deal with at that time. Maybe he was right, in retrospect. Shortly after Charles's death, his sister had a stroke and Noah had his hands full."

The crowd buzzed in monotones as Dianna sat silent, contemplating this new piece in the puzzle of her life. Her face had lost all color—she could feel it. Yet as her mind digested Jessie's words she absently realized that she felt no real shock. Had she always secretly known about Charles? Had these new facts only confirmed what she'd long ago suspected? Funny. She was so calm, so very calm. She turned away from Jessie's sharp questioning eyes, her own darting around the large elegant restaurant furnished with old English paneling and deep red carpeting.

"Are you sure Noah doesn't know?"

"As sure as I can be. As I said, Charles came to Phil so that Noah wouldn't find out, and then Charles died and Phil decided there was no point in telling him."

"I see," she said absently as she realized she had had the key to Charles's behavior all along. She had blotted the events of that night out so well that she had instantly forgotten the mumbled drunken words Charles had muttered to himself. Why? She knew the answer but didn't have the courage to dredge it up and put it into coherent words. Better to forget than acknowledge her own inadequacies.

Jessie continued, calling her back to the present. "I guess what I'm really saying is that Noah has always been a lonely man. He's had to support a family since he was old enough to hold a job. Oh, he's always had women—he's the good-looking, mysterious type, and that alone draws them like bees to honey—not to mention his money. But until the other night at your apartment I have *never* seen him happily content. He deserves and has earned that contentment. Don't let Catherine take that away from either of you. She'll ruin your marriage if you let her—just for the fun of it!" Jessie's eyes bored into Dianna's, hate for Catherine glittering in them.

Dianna smiled. "Don't worry, Jessie. He's been kept so busy lately, I doubt if he's had any free time for our siren." She spoke with conviction, more to put Jessie's mind at rest than to calm her own fears.

Jessie's eyes lit with mischief. "You sly thing, you! You let me rattle out this tale of woe and yet your plans were already mapped out!" She turned serious once more, her eyes showing the concern she felt. "But be careful, Dianna. Don't be taken in by that little-girl attitude of hers. She may look young and naive, but she's at least eighty years old in experience."

"I gather from our conversation that you'd put Catherine number one on a blacklist?" Dianna asked dryly.

"Damn right! She tried her wiles on Philip once. And she did it just to pay Noah back for not giving her enough adulation!"

"Your Philip?"

"Yes, my Philip." Jessie's face mirrored the bitterness of her own story.

"Surely Philip didn't take the bait?"

"Almost," Jessie stated grimly. "Last year I thought I had the perfect life. I had my son, Philip, Junior, two beautiful daughters, a house on the right street in the right neighborhood, the right furnishings, the right clothes, and a husband who was moving up in the world. I played bridge on Tuesdays and Thursdays, tennis on Wednesdays, parties with the right kind of people and a few select friends, Noah included." She glanced up to see Dianna staring at her, perplexed, then took another sip of her drink and continued. "Then one afternoon our son died in an auto accident on his way home from baseball practice with one of the car-pool mothers. It wasn't her fault. P.J. and another boy were killed instantly." She swallowed hard before she continued, ignoring Dianna's muffled exclamation. "I moved like a zombie for weeks afterward. Philip, too."

Now it was Dianna's turn to console and she did. She couldn't even begin to imagine holding together under such a tragedy. If it were Tabby . . .

"Somehow we made it through that first hellish month and everything began slipping into a day-to-day routine, except that there was a hole in our lives that couldn't be filled.

"One day I was going through Phil's closet, cleaning everything in sight just to keep myself from thinking. I pulled out two or three suits and began going through the pockets before sending them to the cleaners. In one suit I found a note and a key to a hotel room. The note was dated a few weeks before P.J. died. I read the note and everything seemed to click into place: Philip's preoccupation at that time, his lack of attention. He had been seeing Catherine at her hotel room for at least two weeks previous to our son's death.''

Jessie took another gulp of her drink as she blinked back a haze of tears.

"My world had already turned topsy-turvy, but at that moment it just stopped. When Philip came home I was sitting on the bed, holding his suit, still wearing my robe. I didn't know where the girls were, I didn't care. I couldn't even cry. I think I had known that everything wasn't right between us, but I thought I could close my eyes and ignore any unpleasantness. When I had to face two tragedies at once, I couldn't cope."

Jessie pushed her drink aside and continued, not wanting Dianna to stop the flow of words. It was a relief to bare her soul after all this time.

"Well, after several weeks of therapy I realized that Philip was only partly to blame for our growing apart. I helped too, by being too busy with my social life to work on our private moments together, and his career made him too tired to take an interest in my life. Catherine came along at just the right time in our lives, and now I believe that anyone would have done. But *she* was there, and she knows just how to build up a male's slightly battered ego. Philip was so overwhelmed to think that someone like her would be interested in him that he fell right into her trap. He didn't realize until later that she was using him to get back at Noah for neglecting her."

"Are you sure that's why Catherine chased him?" Dianna questioned kindly.

"Oh, yes. Catherine made that point very clear. You

see, she hoped I would run to tell Noah and he would get madly jealous. I never did, of course."

"And now both of you are punishing yourselves for something that neither was really to blame for," Dianna mused. "The other night . . ."

Jessie interrupted, her voice firm. "The other night at your home we enjoyed the conversation, the food, the relaxation of being among friends. That doesn't make a marriage."

"Oh, Jessie. I'm so sorry." Dianna's hand covered the other woman's and gave a squeeze. "Please give it time and things will work out—you'll see."

Jessie smiled. "Pollyanna," she retorted softly. "But I've come to my senses lately. I've made up my mind that if I can only keep Philip by holding guilt over him, then I don't want him." She spread her hands on the tablecloth and stared at her plain gold wedding band. "I may never get over the death of my son, but I can't use a child's ghost to keep my husband, and that's what I've been doing."

Dianna looked at Jessie, struck by how different she was today from the pert redhead she had met the other night.

"Sometimes something tragic happens in your life that makes such a big black mark you can't see anything else, Jessie. Because of it you miss all the nice and wonderful things that come your way." Dianna's voice was slow, hesitant, as if she were just discovering the reality of her words for herself. "Don't you think that might be what you're doing?" Now more than ever before she knew her words to be true.

"You're speaking from experience, aren't you?" Jessie's voice was quizzical. "But you're right. That is what

I've been doing." They were silent for a moment, each lost in her own private thoughts.

"You must love Noah very much," Jessie said softly, surprising Dianna.

"He's been wonderful to Tabby and me, and I don't want to hurt him." She chose her words carefully, still wrapped in Jessie's past and her own revelations.

Jessie shook her head at Dianna's evasive answer. "Nonsense."

Dianna laughed with her. "Yes, I love him. Very much," she stated simply.

As they exited the restaurant to go their separate ways, Dianna felt Jessie's hand on her arm. "Dianna? I didn't really mean to talk your ear off. I've never done it before—I just don't know what got into me. But if you ever need anything, please call. I'm awfully glad to have you for a friend."

"Thanks, Jessie. I appreciate that."

A gleam came into Jessie's eyes. "And remember that Noah's your man. Don't let anyone push you around. You've got first claim!"

Dianna laughed. "Right!"

She walked back to the Wescomp building, waving Jimmy and the car back. She had too much to think about and walking would help clear her thoughts. Suddenly she wanted Noah with her. She wanted his arms around her, holding her tight enough to block out all the doubts that were assailing her. She loved him so much! And her love had always been for him, although it had taken her a long time to acknowledge it, even to herself. Catherine had a fight on her hands if she tried anything . . .

The elevator carried her up to the top of the building.

She debated about stopping at Noah's office but thought better of it. Tonight would be soon enough to tell him of her love. They would have dinner by candlelight out on the terrace, put on some soft music, and let nature take its course. She smiled. Funny how things could be so perfect!

10

~~~~~~~~~~~~~~~~~~

She was too preoccupied with her thoughts at first to realize there was someone in the living room with her. Placing her purse on the chair, she turned toward the unexpected sound of tinkling glass. Her look of anticipation at Noah's early arrival instantly turned to one of stunned surprise.

"Don't look so shocked, Mrs. Weston. I know this apartment better than you do. Until two weeks ago I expected to be here permanently."

Catherine continued to stir the tall glass wand around the edge of a crystal martini pitcher, her ice-blue eyes defiantly challenging Dianna. "And as soon as your short reign is over, I'll be back." She took two glasses and poured the mixture equally into both, coming forward to hand one to Dianna. She accepted it without question, not even realizing she was holding it.

Catherine gave a mock salute with her drink. "The first one's for you and the second one's for me." There was a malicious smile in her baby-blue eyes and suddenly Dianna remembered what Jessie had said.

"Are you telling me you're staking a claim for seconds?"

"Of course."

"That shouldn't take more than a forty- or fifty-year wait."

Catherine's eyes narrowed. Her usual barbs were not working. "I want Noah, and I'll get him."

"It's a shame it isn't Christmas. You could ask Santa," Dianna said sweetly. She continued to stand in the middle of the living room, her untouched drink in one hand, her cigarettes in the other. "If I know Mrs. Frank at all, she's called Noah and he should be here any minute. She's not one for divided loyalties, our Mrs. Frank."

Catherine's eyes flickered toward the doorway before she shrugged her shoulders and turned away, her pale-yellow dress hugging the curves of her body as she sat back on the couch, looking more at home there than Dianna.

"Why do you want Noah? For his money?" Dianna asked, suddenly curious about what motivated a woman like Catherine.

Catherine nodded. "It helps, honey. But that isn't the only reason, as I'm sure you've guessed."

"Then why?"

"Because I do. He's what I've always wanted." She glanced down, frowning, but when she looked up at Dianna again, there was a bright light burning in the slyness of her big blue eyes. "You must know as well as I do that as a lover he's superb. So uninhibited, so free with himself, so . . . masculine."

Silence echoed in the room, charging it with electricity as the two women sized each other up. The petite blonde shook her arm and let a small platinum-and-diamond bracelet edge over her wrist to cover the top of one perfectly manicured hand. "Did you see my latest trinket? Your husband sent it to me on your wedding day. I think he wanted to tell me that although he married you he still wants me."

"Really?" Dianna's eyes widened in innocence. "To me it looks more like the perfect payoff for somone who can be bought."

Catherine stared, her facade slipping to expose the hate lurking beneath. "What do you think you've got that can hold a man? My looks are just as good as yours— even better. I've got youth on my side, too. I've even got talent." She stood and slowly walked toward Dianna, stopping to stare at her with hatred in her eyes.

"But I've got Noah. What else would I need?"

"A hold over him. The kid maybe?" She had finally struck home. She watched with delight as the venomous words hit Dianna, leaving her white and then a bright red. "So that's it. I should have known!" She spoke softly, her eyes lighting with sparks of fire. "Is she Noah's? Is that it?"

"Get out," Dianna ordered coldly, quietly.

"Yes, I think I will. The company stinks." Catherine picked up a small bag by the bar and walked slowly across the room, only stopping when she reached the doorway. She turned and looked Dianna up and down. "I didn't give up a year of my life to lose Noah now. I'll get him back. Give me a few days and I'll be snugly nestled in his arms again." Then she was gone.

Dianna sank on to the couch, her legs refusing to hold her anymore. Reaction set in and she trembled all over.

"Dianna? Mrs. Frank called . . ." Noah stood in the doorway, his black brows furrowed together in a frown. He looked so dear, so concerned, so—she began crying, but there was a smile on her lips. Within seconds he was holding her in his arms, cradling her with all the tenderness she had craved earlier. His hand rubbed the back of her neck, curving up to remove the pins from her hair and let the ebony tendrils filter through his fingers. A heaving sigh came from deep within his throat as he pressed his cheek to hers, feeling the slippery dampness of her tears. When he pulled away, her eyes were wide, her bottom lip betraying the tumult of emotions in her breast.

"Catherine was here."

"I hope you said good-bye to her. You'll never see her again."

"She, she . . ."

"She's gone now, darling, and whatever she said that tore at you like this, it was a lie. There is nothing that Catherine could say to you in truth that would upset you."

"But . . ."

"Shhhh," he murmured as his lips came down to claim hers, his hands stroking away frightening images. Slowly her trembling ceased, only to be replaced by another need. His hands sought the curve of her breast, his fingers cupping to tease the nipple gently. Her pulses hammered and he could feel the heavy heartbeat in her chest. He picked her up and carried her to the bedroom, laying her on the bed and covering her with the satin coverlet.

"Noah?"

He sat on the side of the bed, his hand holding hers. There was a dark flickering of light in his eyes that died quickly as he turned away. "You're tired, Dianna— you've been through enough this afternoon. I want you to rest."

"And I want you in bed with me, not holding my hand."

"Are you sure?" he asked quietly, his voice husky and low.

"Please, Noah. I'm sure."

They both undressed, neither speaking except with their eyes. His usually gentle touch had turned into a passionate demand, willing her to respond as she had never before. The thought of losing him was still upper-most in her mind, and she clung to him all the more, holding him closer, wanting to make him a part of her so that he would never be able to leave. She cried in her pleasure, and he licked the tears away, his own need reaching the heights of hers. The momentum increased until she cried out for release, clinging to him as if she were drowning and he was her rock. Afterwards they lay in each other's arms, content with the silence.

Finally his voice invaded her thoughts, his tone soft as velvet. "Dianna?" He stroked the long hair that flowed over the pillow, his eyes searching, waiting for something. An answer to which question? She knew.

She wrapped her arms around his neck, nibbling at his

lower lip. "I love you, Noah Weston. I love you so much I want to burst."

He sighed, catching her close to him again and putting her head on his chest as she adjusted his body to hers. "You're everything I've always wanted. Good, sweet, with just a touch of devil fire and spunk in you to add spice to my dull life." She glanced up to see him grin and he returned her look with love in his eyes. He kissed the tip of her nose. "I've loved you for such a long time, baby. Longer than you'd believe."

"Why didn't you tell me before?"

"Because I wanted you to admit you felt the same." He let his head fall back on the pillow. "It was like pulling teeth to get you to admit anything! I couldn't even get you to agree on the weather!"

"We've wasted so much time." This was home, this was where she belonged. Right on Noah's chest with his arm around her body, holding her close, his less-than-steady heartbeat in her ear. She smiled.

"What's so funny?" He tilted her head up to his view, noting how her hazel eyes glinted with merriment.

"I just decided I want to spend the rest of my life like this, but I don't think your secretary would take too kindly to the idea, to say nothing of your clients."

He chuckled in response before turning serious again. "Dianna, I want to explain about Catherine." His arms gave a light squeeze, keeping her where she was when she would have moved. "I helped her with her career and she helped me by being around when I needed a woman. I had no commitments and didn't want any. She knew that. Then, a few months ago, she started getting possessive. I realized what she was doing and told her it wasn't going to work, but she's persistent if nothing else."

His hand reached up to soothe her back, absently rubbing her skin like a talisman. "Until the night of the cocktail party, I used her as a shield against other women. I knew it and she knew it, but I guess she felt complacent about it. Until you came along. She knew immediately that she was through then, and there was nothing she could do except try to get at me through you."

"I know," she whispered softly, with the conviction of a woman loved.

"You do?" His smoky gray eyes looked down at her, showing his surprise.

"Um-hm. I might have done the same thing in her place. Who knows?"

A muffled laugh rose in his throat. "No, you wouldn't. You'd have run for cover, pronto!" He turned serious again. "I wanted to be fair with her, offer her a share in the record company. But after tonight she'll be gone. She'll never bother either of us again."

"What are you going to do, have her done away with?"

"No. I'm giving her an ultimatum: either she pursues her career somewhere other than Dallas or she won't have a career to pursue."

"What about the trial?"

"It's tomorrow morning. She can stay in a hotel until then. She'll get off with a suspended sentence since it's her first offense."

She raised her hand to his neck and rubbed it against the grain of his beard, stroking the soft skin beneath. He quickly captured it, bringing it to his mouth to press a kiss on her palm, sending shivers up her spine as a warmth grew in her body.

She had to say it again. "I love you, Noah." It was so true. She had always loved him, even when she had run from him. Ever since that first time. His mouth bent to play with hers, teasing her lips open to devour her tongue. He held her tight against his chest and she could feel the hairs tickling her ear as he whispered outrageous love words—things he wanted to do to her, for her, with her. They were both heady with the gift of love each had given the other.

She giggled, running her fingers over his smooth corded back and reveling in the feeling. "I think I'm the one that's supposed to satisfy you, you brute. At least according to every Harold Robbins novel I've ever read."

He smiled complacently. "Good. I was hoping you'd see my side of it. I've always wanted to be teased by small white hands and a mass of curling black hair until I couldn't take any more," he retaliated, softly nibbling her lower lip.

Her eyes twinkled. "That shouldn't take more than a minute or so."

Her hand raked his chest and taut stomach, making him suck in his breath as her touch sent a tingle through his body.

"Oh, so I'm no longer Superman? Well, I'll show you, you little tease!" He began tickling her and they rolled on the bed, carefree laughter bubbling from both throats until suddenly their needs flared to consume them both and the caresses began in earnest.

It was very late afternoon by the time Noah was dressed and ready to return to the office. He bent over Dianna, who was still cuddled in the soft comforter, sleepy and content.

"I won't be long, honey. I've just got to wind up some

unfinished business. You get a little rest." His lips touched her forehead, his hand strayed to give her a small intimate squeeze, and she answered with a sleepy smile.

But as tired as she was, her mind continued to churn with thoughts and questions brought up during the emotion-packed day. Should she tell Noah about Tabby's parentage? She knew Noah would be just as happy as she was over the fact that he was already the natural parent they both wanted him to be.

Still, the news was bound to come as a shock, and for that reason alone she hesitated to break it to him. She hated to do anything just now to rock her boat. The newfound contentment of their life together was too precious to risk in any way. After all, wasn't it possible that Noah would think she had purposely hidden the information from him? Perhaps he would even suspect that she had collaborated with June to take advantage of the guilt he felt over his brother's crime! Dianna shook her head with a smile.

After all they'd been through together, she didn't think Noah would jump to that conclusion. Yet the fact remained that she had always suspected Tabby was Noah's child. Why had she never admitted it, not even to herself?

She realized now that her attitude had been formed almost unconsciously seven years ago. It had begun during those few nights of ecstasy she had known with Noah after the rape. In the delirium of his lovemaking she had known no inhibitions or doubts, but with the cold light of dawn each day, worry and self-recrimination had returned to plague her. Brought up by a strict and moralistic mother, she had been taught that pleasure was the root of all evil, and so she began to fear that the delight she felt in Noah's arms was somehow sinful.

Her doubts were brought to a head one day when she happened to overhear Noah talking on the phone as she passed his study door.

". . . and find a house somewhere, Phil. A nice one. I don't want her to have to worry about where she'll be staying for the time being. Set up a bank account, make it an automatic payment of two thousand a month for now. I'll handle the details on this end. Right. See you later." The phone clicked and she had run into the bathroom, her heart unwilling to admit what she had just heard but knew to be true. She was being paid off! Oh, God! The terrible ache of another loss consumed her.

Later that morning she had dressed and left the penthouse. She had never pressed charges against Charles, preferring to disappear from view completely. She never wanted to have to face Noah Weston again, understanding for the first time a bitter truth: though Charles had perpetrated a crime against her, it was his brother who had caused the more lasting psychological damage.

Now, seven years later, she consciously knew what she had always unconsciously felt—that Noah was the father of Tabby and that Tabby had been conceived in a love she had denied so that she would be able to live with her own puritan conscience. It was one thing to have a child that had been forced on her in a situation over which she had no control. It was quite another to bear a child out of wedlock and admit that it was the result of her own passionate attraction to a man who was not her husband. Her mother would have been proved right; she would have had to see herself as wanton and loose-moraled, deserving of the scorn her parents had heaped upon her.

The phone jangled and she jumped, coming back to the present with a start.

"Mrs. Weston?" a male voice questioned.

"This is she."

"This is Dr. Storn. I'm calling to give you some good news. Tabby is finishing the last series of tests and everything is just the way it should be. She can go home the day after tomorrow."

"That's wonderful! Are you sure?"

"Positive. She should stay in town for another six weeks for checkups, but she can resume a regular routine, just like any other little six-year-old. I understand she's anxious to get well fast because she's going to be visiting a ranch where she'll ride a hundred horses a day!" he announced with a tinge of laughter.

"Her father promised her a pony to ride as soon as she was well," Dianna chuckled.

"Well, that did the trick. Some of these tests weren't easy, but the thought of a pony carried her through. If I could try the same tactics on some of my adult patients, I would. It works wonders. Everyone needs something good to look forward to."

Minutes later she was dressed and applying a light touch of make-up. She had to tell Noah the news. It was wonderful to feel this way, so alive. And suddenly she had so much to look forward to. All thanks to Noah. She had Noah and he loved her. Everything was roses and champagne.

Catherine's machinations had backfired completely. Instead of driving them further apart as she had apparently hoped, her actions had brought them together. Funny how changeable human emotions were. Charles,

Catherine: they were a part of the past, and she would never again dwell there. Not now. The future was so bright it blinded her to all that was behind her. She smiled as she brushed her hair, leaving it down and flowing on her shoulders. Noah would be as happy about Tabby as she was. . . .

11

～ღღღღღღღ～

Glad you came on time, Catherine. I'm not in the habit of making idle threats." Noah stood and circled the desk, an envelope in his hand. "Everything you need is in here. Reservations for your trip back to Nashville, the confirmation at the Hilton for tonight, and money for your expenses. Your trial is tomorrow. Phil will meet you and take care of that end of things." His eyes narrowed, taking in the hard, empty look in her eyes and the crimson lips set in a stiff smile. She looked like a painted china doll, all pretty and sweet with nothing inside but cotton stuffing. She was the perfect antithesis of his

Dianna—so warm and loving, and totally his. "Any questions?"

"Yes, one." Her smile grew broader but it never seemed to reach her eyes. "Why did you marry *her* while I was here? What can she give you that I can't?"

He gave no sign of surprise at her brusqueness, excusing it when he realized she had no choice. She had already tried everything else. "You and I were never close, Catherine, and we both know it," he said quietly. "The best way for this to end is for you to bow out gracefully."

Catherine took a deep breath and plunged in. She still had a piece of ammunition, the information she had startled out of Dianna that afternoon. It had to work. It had to! "Was it because you wanted custody of your own daughter and the mother came as part of the package?" she questioned sweetly.

"What are you talking about?" His voice was soft but his manner was immediately that of a poised fighter, ready to take a jab. She smiled, suddenly confident. She was ready.

"It's true, isn't it? The proud and upright leader of Dallas society is the father of an illegitimate child!" Her hand claimed his arm, giving it a squeeze. "But don't worry, darling. I won't tell anybody, and we can go on the way we were always meant to. Poor dear—forced into marriage just because you wanted your own child." Her fingers teased his firm jaw. "If I'd known you wanted a chip off the old block so bad, I would have obliged you, darling. We could still adopt yours, if you wanted . . ." His hand grabbed hers and placed it on the top of the desk in chilling rebuff.

"And what makes you think I was forced into this,

Kitty?" he asked conversationally as he leaned his hips against the edge of the desk, crossing his arms and staring at her with cold steel-gray eyes that seemed to deflate her like a pinprick in a balloon.

"Well, I . . ."

"Don't you think there are any of a dozen different ways I could have gone about getting my daughter if that was all I wanted? Assuming your suspicions are correct, of course."

"Oh, they're correct, all right. Your sweet little wife turned white at the mention of it this afternoon." She watched his brow furrow at her words. Then she walked to the window and turned to face him again. "But I'd make a better wife for you than she would. I'm what you need. You lead too fast a life for her. She's more the stay-at-home type. You'll be bored out of your skull in no time." She threw back her head, knowing her hair sparkled bright gold as the afternoon sun filtered through it, making a halo to frame her face. "We make a good pair, Noah."

She moistened her lips and slowly opened the first three buttons of the tight silk button-down dress she wore. Her full, unbound breasts were almost totally exposed and she stood before him in a blatantly provocative pose.

"Remember that time in New York when we were up all night making love?" Her voice turned to a husky whisper.

"That's all there is, Catherine—memories of sex, not love. Don't get the two confused." Noah's voice was grim as he stalked over to the window. "Now button your dress and get the hell out of here. Don't make an even bigger fool of yourself." He watched in astonish-

ment as she grinned, leaning over his desk and pushing
the intercom buzzer that would call his secretary.

"What the . . . ?" He stopped in midstride, confused
at her actions as she ran into his opened arms, hugging
his waist as she pressed her body to his. Reflexes
demanded he hold her and his arms circled her shoulders
for balance just as the door opened to frame his shocked
secretary. Immediately it all became clear.

"Why, you little . . . !" he growled, his gray eyes
steeling to hatred. But before he had a chance to wrench
himself away from Catherine's grasping hold he heard a
gasp and knew with a certainty that his secretary wasn't
the only one watching the well-planned scene.

He could see the raw pain in Dianna's eyes, the
expression of betrayal etched into the pale transparency
of her skin.

Her hands clenched into fists as she stared, fascinated,
at the silhouetted scene before her. Logic screamed *no* in
her brain, but her heart felt as though it were breaking
just the same.

"This little scene was staged beautifully, Catherine. I
must congratulate you," Noah said tautly before he
pushed her out of his arms and took a step toward
Dianna. "Are you going to give her the satisfaction of
believing it?"

Dianna stared at Noah as if seeing him for the first time.
Her glance then flickered to Catherine, seeing the trium-
phant smile poised on her lips. Noah took another step
toward her, but she held up her hand to ward him off.

"No!"

"Dianna, after everything that happened this afternoon, do you believe this?"

A vision of the afternoon flashed through her mind.

Noah's lean hard body curved to hers, his hand gently cupping her breast in possessive intimacy, his breath soft on her neck. His words of declared love. She looked at him again. No! This couldn't be the same Noah. He wouldn't have left her arms for another woman. He couldn't!

She glanced back at Catherine; the other woman was watching her with a satisfied feline look. Dianna stood taller. She wasn't going to let Noah go so easily!

"No, I don't believe it," she stated quietly. "But I would like an explanation." Let me be right, she prayed. Let Noah tell me the truth.

"The truth, you little fool, is that your husband still wants me. No matter what he says . . ."

"Shut up and get out of here, Catherine. Now!" Noah's barely leashed anger was plainly visible.

Catherine realized she had lost, but the alley cat in her continued to fight. She slowly, provocatively began buttoning her blouse. "Perhaps you two do deserve each other after all. What a pair you are! One is a tramp trying to act respectable and the other is a father who won't even publicly recognize his own child!" Blue eyes glistened with defiance and hate. She watched Dianna turn white at her words and knew that even in losing there was a victory.

"Shut up!" Noah took a step closer to her and Catherine backed off. For the first time she was afraid of him. "You have a foul mouth, Kitty. I'll see that you never sing again, anywhere, if I ever hear that rumor."

"Really, Noah. I can't be the only one who knows." She gave a slight, high-pitched giggle. "Probably half the town is in on your little secret."

"You don't know a damn thing! Now get out of here

and don't ever let me see you again. Ever!" Noah stood in the center of the room as he watched Catherine reach for her purse in a nervous gesture and march, head high and a smirk on her face, out the door past his wife and secretary. His secretary raised a brow at Noah and he gave a silent nod in communication. She left, following Catherine to make sure she was on the elevator and out of the building.

"Dianna."

She stared at him, seeing the happiness she had felt only moments ago fleeing away, never to return. Now Noah knew he was Tabby's father, and he would hate her for never having told him. Wasn't he angry already?

"Come in and close the door," he finally said wearily, running a hand through his hair. "We don't have to have the whole office hear us."

Like an automaton, she did as she was told, standing just inside the room and waiting in stoic silence for him to accuse her of keeping the identity of his own child a secret. She couldn't keep her eyes away from him. It was like watching a giant storm brewing, knowing that destruction would follow. But she was unable to run.

Suddenly the room was filled with a tight silence. She wished he wasn't silhouetted by the bright light from the large picture window. She wanted to see his face. Her hand reached for the contours of his cheek before she let her arm fall lifelessly to her side. He took it, holding it next to his heart. She could feel the erratic beat and it sent shivers through her.

"I'm sorry, Noah. I'm so sorry." Her voice was barely a whisper.

"So you finally decided to admit it?"

"Yes."

"All this time. I waited all this time and you never said a word."

"You . . . you knew?" she stammered, unable to believe that Noah had pretended to be Tabby's uncle all the while knowing she was really his daughter. "But how? And why? Why didn't *you* ever say anything?"

"I've known that Charles was sterile for years, Dianna. So when I learned of Tabby's existence and found out from June that you'd never seen other men, I knew she was mine. What I couldn't understand was your reluctance to admit it. At first I thought that you genuinely believed Charles was Tabby's father. But I sensed a conflict in you—a problem that you had to resolve before you could face the truth. You did know, didn't you?"

"Yes. He muttered something about it that night, but I was trying so hard to block out the memory of the rape that the words went with it." She sighed and he allowed her hand to drop, leaving her cold and chilled. Suddenly she was exhausted.

"But instead of blocking out Charles, you blocked out our nights together."

"Yes. I couldn't accept the responsibility of it. I had to be pregnant as the result of the rape. If I was pregnant with your child, then I had to take responsibility for the pregnancy, and I couldn't do that. My values at that time wouldn't allow me to acknowledge that I had become an unwed mother of my own free will." She started to walk to the chair, but her legs gave way. She crumpled to the floor, leaning against the back of the desk, staring at the hands that lay so quietly in her lap.

"Why did you leave me, Dianna?" His voice came

from far across the room—hollow, bodyless. It was better that way, easier to talk, to say what she felt.

"Because of the phone call."

"What phone call?"

"I overheard a phone call you made to Philip. You were arranging a house and allowance for me—sweeping me under the carpet—and I couldn't take it. I had to run before I lost any more shreds of my self-respect. I couldn't handle the fact that you had slept with me, murmured words I thought meant you loved me, and then decided to set me up in a house you could visit when the urge hit you. I had fallen in love with you and thought you could never love me in return because of what Charles had done. I couldn't stand it. I left and tried to cover my tracks as quickly as I could. Then, when I found out I was pregnant, I couldn't face the fact that you were the cause. I had given myself to you freely and you had rejected me. I blamed it on Charles."

He sighed heavily. "So that was it," he murmured more to himself than to her. "I thought I had frightened you with my love. I had no idea why else you would have run away unless you hated me." She didn't hear him move but suddenly he was in front of her, kneeling on the floor in order to look her in the eye. Two fingers lifted her tear-stained cheeks to his scrutiny.

"Charles was the youngest in my family, spoiled by both my sister and myself. We wanted to give him everything we never had. When I was in high school I worked for his first bike, my sister kept hens so she could sell the eggs for good clothes that would make him feel as well dressed as the other kids in school.

"By the time he was fifteen, we had a real problem on

our hands. His escapades were renowned throughout the countryside. He thought all he had to do was ask for money and it would drop like manna from heaven.

"When Charles found out he was sterile, it was a great shock to him. First he went to Philip, then he finally came to me. We had been discussing it the day I interviewed you for a job seven years ago. Then, that night, he talked you into going on a date with him. I think he took his frustration out on you. It doesn't excuse him, Dianna, but I've often wondered just how big a part I played in what happened. He had always come to me for help and this was one time I could do nothing."

He kissed her tenderly on the forehead before continuing.

"After the rape, Charles had gone to stay at the ranch with my sister, Honey. The day before you left she called to say she couldn't find him. Naturally, I thought he was hiding from us because of what had happened. I never intended, by the way, to protect him from the law. I should have known better than to expect him to have a guilty conscience. He had picked up another girl, one more willing, and they spent several days together painting the town before he had that accident." His voice grew hoarse. "I wanted to hold on to you, but first I had to straighten out the family mess. That was why I was arranging for a house you could live in. I wanted you safe until everything was back in control, then I wanted to marry you. I loved you then, Dianna, just as I love you now."

"Even after Charles?"

He nodded. "It didn't make any difference to me, darling. In fact, I loved you more because I couldn't hurt for you." He smiled sadly, stroking back a stray lock of her hair. "Even when you were yelling at me like a virago."

"Then why didn't you tell me, instead of making me believe you married me because of Tabby?"

"Because I thought *I* had scared you away, not the telephone call. I thought if I brought you here to live, then perhaps you'd grow to love me too."

"And I did."

He nodded. "Despite Catherine."

She gave a little sob. She didn't know whether to laugh or cry. "And now can we live happily ever after?"

"Now," he stated firmly, "we move to the ranch, where we will raise cows, and chickens, and children. And not necessarily in that order."

"But what about Wescomp?"

"I sold it."

"But why? I thought you loved the company."

"I want to bring up our children away from this rat race. I was in the process of selling the company when I married you and then Catherine's arrest interfered. The press had already linked her to me and I didn't want any adverse publicity or the stock might have fluctuated." He grinned.

"Believe me, darling, we'll be gentlemen farmers. I enjoy the ranch, but I don't really have to work by the sweat of my brow for a living anymore. Now I want to spend time with my wife and my daughter, and enjoy life."

His lips softly touched hers, coaxing, pleading, and she responded with all the love that overflowed from her heart.

"Think you can start again as a lady of leisure and my

wife? No more lies or deceptions between us?" he asked, a tender note in his voice.

She nodded, her smile growing bigger as happiness grew inside.

He stood up, putting out his hands and slowly drawing her up and into the comfort of his embrace. Her arms crept around his neck, softly playing with his hair, feeling the texture and vitality of it.

"We'll start again," she promised. "I think it's time you got busy with the rest of our family. Tabby can't be an only child forever."

12

ᵕᵕᵕᵕᵕᵕᵕᵕᵕᵕᵕ

Dianna lounged in the hammock on the large shaded
rear patio of the ranch house. She smiled as she sipped
her iced tea. Some ranch house! It resembled more
closely the large hacienda of a terribly important don in
the south of Mexico. The house was the shape of an H
with both front and back patios enclosed by a large white
stucco wall. The front patio was all garden, complete with
it's own double fountain, while the rear patio circled the
rectangular swimming pool. A large wooden gate stood
in the center back wall leading out to the other buildings
on the ranch. The stable was directly in line with the rear

of the house and Dianna could hear the faint whinny of the horses as they pulled in from the cattle pens. Noah was out there today, taking a stock count.

She stretched her toes and pulled her arms over her head, completely drugged with the happiness she had known these past eight weeks since she had come here with Noah. It was amazing how wonderful it felt to belong, truly belong, to someone you loved. Her tan jeans stretched over slim legs and she chuckled to herself as the button above her zipper tautened over the faint rounding of her stomach.

Honey's voice broke the silence. "Well, the last of the packing is done and in the morning I'll be ready to vacate." She slumped in a chair directly across from Dianna. She was a woman well into her forties, with hair already beginning to grey and a pleasantly plump figure. Her face was creased with lines that told the story of many days in the sun and a tendency toward nearsightedness. There was no trace of the stroke she'd endured seven years ago. She grinned broadly at Dianna. "I guess you won't feel too badly being deserted like this, will you?"

"I just don't see why you and Frank can't live here, Honey. After all, it's your home too, and in much better repair than the old homestead."

"You're a doll, and I love you, but I want a little privacy for my new husband and myself, even if we have known each other for years. After all, I'll only be down the road a ways. We'll see each other more often than you think!" she laughed, and her light gray eyes lit up at the mention of her future husband. He had been the foreman of the ranch for the past ten years and it had taken him the last three to convince Honey he was the only man for her. "Just 'cause there's snow on the roof . . ." She plucked a lock of gray hair and raised her eyebrows, making Dianna chuckle again. "Besides, you two need to have some privacy, too." She glanced at Dianna's middle. "Have you told Noah, yet?"

Absolute delight filtered through Dianna. "That he's going to be a proud papa? Yes, I told him last night. He didn't seem to be at all surprised."

Honey grinned. "Why should he be—he's been working on it ever since you two got married!" They both giggled as Dianna blushed becomingly.

"Anyway, we're going to wait and tell Tabby a little later. Seven months is a long time for a child to wait for a brother or sister."

The back gate opened and Noah strode in, his boots thumping on the concrete as he walked around the pool to the canopied patio, his eyes shining as he grinned at both of them. He took his hat off and wiped his brow with his sleeve. He looked tired and dusty and gorgeous.

"I'll go get some more iced tea," Honey said to no one in particular as she stood and ambled toward the large sliding glass doors.

"Make mine a beer." Noah sat down next to Dianna, his hand holding hers as his lips brushed her hair. "How's the little mother today?" His skin had darkened from the harsh east Texas sun and his eyes crinkled in the corners. His grin widened as he pointedly glanced at Dianna's stomach.

"Doing fine and waiting for you with good news. Jessie called and she and Philip are accepting our invitation to spend next weekend with us. I told them we'd send the plane to Love Field in Dallas to pick them up Friday morning. They're taking the girls out of school for the day."

"Good. It'll do both of them good to have a change of scene. Maybe they'll take a better look at what they've got and both of them will come to their senses."

Dianna hooted. "And they call women devious match-makers!"

"Well," Noah said laughingly, "I know it's impossible for anyone to be as happy as I am when I've got you under control, but I'd like my friends to be at least half as happy."

"What do you mean, when you've got me 'under control,' Mr. Weston!" she asked in mock anger.

"You *are* the person that bought five bushels of apples at the market, then didn't have the recipe for apple sauce, or jars, or paraffin, aren't you?" His brow rose and a lazy mocking smile turned up the corners of his mouth.

"It takes time to get the hang of everything. Besides, you said you loved apples."

His hand slid behind her waist, lifting her into his lap with one deceptively easy movement. "I love my wife more, and if it pleases her to play Eve and tempt me with apples, then I'll eat the damn things. Just as soon as I'm sated with her." He murmured the words lovingly as he nibbled on her ear, making bursts of electricity sing through her veins.

"And you promise you won't get tired of me, even when I'm big and grumpy?"

"I'll never get tired of you, Dianna. Never." He spoke softly, earnestly, his eyes probing hers. "This child and all others we have are going to have their father where he should be: at their mother's side so I can watch them grow even before they are born as well as after." He smoothed her hair back and kissed the tip of her nose before continuing. "I missed so much with Tabby. I don't ever want that to happen again."

"It won't," she promised, knowing that this was the way it should be, the beginning of a dream come true.

Silhouette Desire
15-Day Trial Offer
A new romance series
that explores
contemporary relationships
in exciting detail

Four Silhouette Desire romances, free for 15 days!
We'll send you four new Silhouette Desire romances
to look over for 15 days, absolutely free! If you decide
not to keep the books, return them and owe nothing.

Four books a month, free home delivery. If you like
Silhouette Desire romances as much as we think you
will, keep them and return your payment with the
invoice. Then we will send you four new books every
month to preview, just as soon as they are published.
You pay only for the books you decide to keep, and
you never pay postage and handling.

Coming Next Month

Not Even For Love by Erin St. Claire

When a misunderstanding threatened to drive them apart, the memory of their passion drove Jordan to convince Reeves of the truth. His misty green eyes and sensual mouth had lifted her to peaks of ecstasy she could never forget.

Make No Promises by Sherry Dee

Even though Cassie was engaged to another man, she was instantly attracted to Steele Malone. He waged a passionate war on her senses, defying her emotions and lulling her body with primitive pleasures.

Moment In Time by Suzanne Simms

She knew Tyler expected a man to build his treasured dam, but Carly was a fully qualified civil engineer. What began as a battle of wills blazed anew in the Santa Fe sunset, a flashfire passion which consumed them both.

Whenever I Love You by Alana Smith

Diana Nolan was Treneau Cosmetics' new goddess of beauty. Paul Treneau was the boss who whisked her away to his Hawaiian paradise for "business." But she had ignited in him a spark of desire fated to burn out of control.

YOU'LL BE SWEPT AWAY
WITH SILHOUETTE DESIRE

$1.75 each

1 ☐ CORPORATE AFFAIR
Stephanie James

2 ☐ LOVE'S SILVER WEB
Nicole Monet

3 ☐ WISE FOLLY
Rita Clay

4 ☐ KISS AND TELL
Suzanne Carey

5 ☐ WHEN LAST WE LOVED
Judith Baker

6 ☐ A FRENCHMAN'S KISS
Kathryn Mallroy

Silhouette Desire

Now Available

Corporate Affair by Stephanie James

Kalinda had come to Colorado determined to
avenge a lost love. But she was shaken by
Rand Alastair who conquered and
claimed her wounded heart.

Love's Silver Web by Nicole Monet

When Jace's lips, hot and passionate, came down
on hers, Laura was overwhelmed with desire.
It was just a matter of time before he
possessed her, body and soul.

Wise Folly by Rita Clay

Seven years had not dimmed Diana's desire for
Noah. How could she deny him now, when he
gave her everything she ever longed for
and more?

Kiss And Tell by Suzanne Carey

Jenna tried to free her mind of Duke Tyrell. But
one moonlit night haunted her, when Duke
had captured her heart and mesmerized
her senses with love.

When Last We Loved by Judith Baker

Even the glitter and flash of Nashville's country
music world couldn't compete with the dizzying
rapture Cassie felt in Hoyt Temple's arms.

A Frenchman's Kiss by Kathryn Mallory

In the dark, ripe fields of grapes that stretched
out around them, Jean Paxton abandoned
herself to the searing kisses of a Frenchman
who made her forget . . .

Dear Reader:
Please take a few moments to fill out this questionnaire. It will help us give you more of the Desires you'd like best.

Mail to: **Karen Solem**
Silhouette Books
1230 Ave. of the Americas, New York, N.Y. 10020

1. How did you obtain **WISE FOLLY?**

10-1 ☐ **Bookstore**
-2 ☐ **Supermarket**
-3 ☐ **Variety/discount store**
-4 ☐ **Department store**
-5 ☐ **Drug store**

-6 ☐ **Newsstand**
-7 ☐ **Airport**
-8 ☐ **Book Club**
-9 ☐ **From a friend**
-0 ☐ **Other:** _____
(write in)

2. How many Silhouette Desires have you read including this one?
(circle one number) 11- **1 2 3 4 5 6**

3. Overall how would you rate this book?

12-1 ☐ **Excellent** -2 ☐ **Very good**
-3 ☐ **Good** -4 ☐ **Fair** -5 ☐ **Poor**

4. Which elements did you like best about this book?

13-1 ☐ **Heroine** -2 ☐ **Hero** -3 ☐ **Setting** -4 ☐ **Story line**
-5 ☐ **Love scenes** -6 ☐ **Ending** -7 ☐ **Other Characters**

5. Do you prefer love scenes that are

14-1 ☐ **Less explicit than in this book**
-2 ☐ **More explicit than in this book**
-3 ☐ **About as explicit as in this book**

6. What influenced you most in deciding to buy this book?

15-1 ☐ **Cover** -2 ☐ **Title** -3 ☐ **Back cover copy**
-4 ☐ **Recommendations** -5 ☐ **You buy all Silhouette Books**

7. How likely would you be to purchase other Silhouette Desires in the future?

16-1 ☐ **Extremely likely**
-2 ☐ **Somewhat likely**
-3 ☐ **Not very likely**
-4 ☐ **Not at all likely**

8. Have you been reading...

17-1 ☐ **Only Silhouette Romances**
-2 ☐ **Mostly Silhouette Romances**
-3 ☐ **Mostly one other romance** _____
(write one in)
-4 ☐ **No one series of romance in particular**

9. Please check the box next to your age group.

18-1 ☐ **Under 18** -3 ☐ **25-34** -5 ☐ **50-54**
-2 ☐ **18-24** -4 ☐ **35-49** -6 ☐ **55 +**

10. Would you be interested in receiving a romance newsletter? If so please fill in your name and address.

Name _____

Address _____

City _____ State _____ Zip _____

19 ___ 20 ___ 21 ___ 22 ___ 23 ___